ACCEPTED

PARA-MILITARY RECRUITER™ BOOK 03

RENÉE JAGGÉR

MICHAEL ANDERLE

THE ACCEPTED TEAM

Thanks to the Beta Readers
Malyssa Brannon, Rachel Beckford, John Ashmore, Kelly
O'Donnell, David Laughlin

Thanks to the JIT Readers
Christopher Gilliard
Zacc Pelter
Diane L. Smith
Dave Hicks
Wendy L Bonell
Dorothy Lloyd
Jan Hunnicutt
Paul Westman

Editor
The SkyFyre Editing Team

The vampire on Julie's doorstep kept his polite smile fixed in place. "May I come in?" he prompted.

Julie's mouth opened and shut a few times. Not because Julius Nox was a vampire. She'd gotten used to them. He was the head of the vampire royal family, though. That was concerning.

"Um, hi," she squeaked.

The corners of Julius' eyes crinkled, but he said nothing more.

What is King Daddy Vampire doing at my door? Julie opened her mouth again, then looked at Julius' pricey leather shoes, the toes almost touching her threshold. Wasn't there something about inviting vampires in?

The legend that claims that vampires must be invited into homes to cross the threshold is pure myth, a tiny voice supplied in her mind.

"Miss Meadows?" Julius arched an elegant eyebrow.

"I'm sorry," Julie blurted, stumbling backward and opening the door wider. "Please, uh, come inside." Despite what her training, which hovered just below her subconscious, had just told her, she assumed it was polite to invite him in.

"Thank you very much." Julius gave an eloquent half-bow and stepped into the apartment.

Julie felt her cheeks warm as she closed the door and took in the elegant vampire king in the middle of her tiny apartment. It still smelled of stale gasoline, and the whole thing would fit in less than half of Julius Nox's study at his mansion in Staten Island. An open-plan kitchenette and little living space, a narrow bed pushed up against the far wall under the window that overlooked the narrow street. Worse, the remnants of a day spent recovering at home were scattered all over the apartment: plates and mugs in the sink, scones going stale on the counter, the bed rumpled and unmade, and a book lying open on the nightstand beside a colorful beanie.

Julie scrambled past Julius to pull out one of the two chairs at the tiny kitchen table. "Um, Sire, please, uh, sit."

Julius obeyed, then folded his manicured hands over his crossed legs. Julie straightened her bedspread and scooped up the beanie, then clutched it with both hands. Did he know she was holding one of the most magical artifacts in the paranormal world? His eyes were on it.

You're still wearing your unicorn slippers, the beanie told her unhelpfully.

Julie tossed him onto the bed for bringing that regrettable detail to her attention. She straightened her bathrobe with all the dignity she could muster. "Would you like some coffee, Sire?"

"That would be very nice, thank you." Julius smiled.

Julie switched on the coffee machine. "It's not fancy or anything," she managed. Her cheeks felt even warmer. He was an actual king. Was she even supposed to give him coffee? Did he have food tasters or something? Did she have any garlic in the house? She thought there was some on the pizza base in her freezer. *Crap!*

"I get quite enough of fanciness in my life." Julius winked. "Please sit, Miss Meadows."

"My apartment is in a state." Julie shoved the scones into the bread bin. "Sorry."

"No matter. I'm sorry for dropping by so late and so unexpectedly." Julius gestured at the other chair. "I understand you were hurt in the altercation last night."

Julie's head still ached dully through the Tylenol she'd taken earlier. She sat down while the coffee machine whirred and hissed. Julius glanced at Hat, still in his colorful beanie form on the bed.

"Uh, about last night." Julie intertwined her fingers in her lap. "I didn't mean for Malcolm to get hurt. I really didn't think there would be a fight."

Julius sighed. "There's no need to apologize for my son's actions, Miss Meadows. I don't think you could have stopped him if you tried."

"I feel like I should have tried, though, Sire. He was bent on going after that Yeti." Julie bit off the end of her sentence before she blurted, "to impress you."

Julius sat back in his seat, mouth twisting in a wry smile. "Malcolm is going to make mistakes. It's part of growing into the leader he has to become. I just regret that you were hurt in his latest escapade."

"That was my choice, Sire." Julie smirked. "It's not Malcolm's fault."

"Maybe not."

The coffee machine beeped. Julie got up and poured two mugs. "Cream, Sire? Sugar?"

"Neither, thank you." Julius took his mug in an elegant hand and sipped.

Julie did her best not to stare at the vampire king drinking coffee from a mug with a design of a playful kitten with a ball of yarn on it. "Is Malcolm okay?"

"Oh, yes. Dr. Olena healed him." Julius shrugged. "He's up in his room, playing that dreadful video game again."

"You know, Sire, Malcolm did his best to protect Taylor and

me in that sewer." Julie hesitated. "I know he is impetuous, but he's a really good guy."

"Of that, I'm well aware, Miss Meadows." Julius set the mug down. "And you don't have to look so nervous. I'm not here because you're in any kind of trouble."

Julie met his eyes. They were blood-red around the pupil, gradually turning black at the outer edge of the iris, and completely unflinching. She wondered how much power Julius Nox had in the paranormal world, then reflected that he made even her boss, who had the ability to transform into a four-hundred-pound tiger, nervous.

Still, she'd liked Julius the first time she met him, and she rebelled at kowtowing to him.

"Then why are you here?" She kept her gaze steady.

Julius' lip twitched again. "Since you ask so boldly, I'll answer the same way." He took another sip of his coffee. "The truth is, Miss Meadows, you have a remarkable tendency to pop up wherever there is trouble. My son does the same thing."

Julie wanted to deny it but couldn't.

"I don't think that is a bad thing." Julius gave her a steady look over the rim of his mug, steam rippling in front of his bright red eyes. "You have been making waves ever since you joined the OPMA, and that hasn't been long."

"What, because I'm human?" Julie folded her arms.

"No, it's not just that." Julius shrugged. "With Queen Esmerelda getting older, the Eternity Throne's fate in question, and the seven royal families at loggerheads, the paranormal world is ripe for change. I think you will be a force behind some of that change."

"Maybe some things about the paranormal world *need* to change." Julie raised an eyebrow.

Julius raised a placating hand. "I'm not arguing with you, Miss Meadows. I agree with you. Malcolm considers you a friend. It is a title he doesn't give to many. Well, not many people he meets in real life, anyway." A sigh escaped the vampire's lips. "My son is at a malleable age. Easily influenced. If you're going to be part of his life, I wanted to get a measure of you in your own environment." His eyes flashed around the apartment.

Julie's cheeks reddened. "It's normally not this messy."

Julius chuckled. "Oh, I wouldn't worry about that if I were you. It's not as though you have an army of cleaners armed with magical spells."

A cleaning spell? That sounded like a useful piece of magic. Julie refrained from saying so, sipping her coffee instead. "Malcolm really values your opinion of him, you know."

"As he should." Julius sighed, but the corners of his eyes crinkled at the mention of his son's name. "He doesn't see that he has the capacity to become one of the greatest leaders the Nox family has ever produced."

Julie blinked. "Maybe you should tell him that."

"And inflate his young head to even greater proportions?" Julius chuckled. "Malcolm has grown up as the heir to one of the most powerful thrones in the paranormal world. It's important that he respects that and learns not to squander everything my family has built over many generations."

Julie took another sip of her coffee. "I wouldn't worry about *Malcolm* doing that."

Julius raised an eyebrow. "I assume you're referring to my son's choice of bride."

Julie huffed. She didn't want to get eaten by an angry vampire, or she would have scoffed.

"Spit it out, Miss Meadows." Julius' lips twitched, a smile almost escaping. "I can see you have an opinion of Cassidy."

Julie put her mug down and folded her arms. "Fine, Sire. You *did* ask."

Julius gestured broadly with one hand.

"She's speciesist, possessive, a total drama queen, and incredibly rude and entitled." Julie ticked the flaws off on her fingers as she spoke. "She treats me like crap because I'm a human, and she treats Malcolm like she owns him. If I were you, I'd be madder about Malcolm wanting to marry her than the Yeti thing."

Julie stopped and watched the vampire warily. *Did I just cross a line?*

Julius gazed at her in silence for a second, then chuckled. "That pretty much sums up my future daughter-in-law." He took a long sip of his coffee.

"I don't even know if Malcolm loves her." Julie lowered her hands into her lap. "He seems to think marrying her will impress you."

"That's bold of you to say, Miss Meadows, but there's no denying that the political alliance the marriage will create is advantageous." Julius sighed. "I told Malcolm that shouldn't be the only reason to engage in a union, but he didn't listen." He shrugged. "As I said before, my son is free to make his own choices."

Julie looked down at her hands. "I didn't mean to be disrespectful."

"Not at all." Julius smiled. "It's refreshing to hear someone speak their mind to me. People find me intimidating." He finished his coffee and set the mug down. "Thank you for the coffee."

"Uh, anytime." Julie glanced at him. "Thanks for coming over."

"I won't trouble you any longer. You're a little on the pale side, and that's coming from a vampire." Julius winked as he rose to his feet. "I think you should get back to bed and that book you're reading. It's a good one."

"Thank you, Sire." Julie got up and took the mugs to the sink.

Julius was at the doorway, his hand on the knob, but he turned back to her. "Miss Meadows, I have said many times that Malcolm is free to make his own mistakes, but rest assured that I believe your presence in his life is not one of them." He flashed her a last fanged smile and was gone.

Julie heard the roar of a powerful engine as the vampire drove away. She hurried over to the window but only spotted taillights turning off the street and disappearing into Bay Ridge. "Well, that was weird."

"He likes you." The colorful beanie sat up and jumped onto the nightstand. "And if you throw me like an old sock again, I'll turn into a mosquito and buzz around your head all night."

"I'll swat you." Julie slid back into bed, kicking off her unicorn slippers. "Do you think Julius knew you were…well, you?"

"I wouldn't worry about it."

Julie glared at him. "What's that supposed to mean?"

Hat was as silent as if he were an ordinary beanie made of wool. Julie rolled her eyes. "Fine. Keep your secrets." She pulled her covers up to her chin and puffed up her pillow but didn't reach for her book. "Hey, Hat?"

The beanie's pom-pom turned to her. "What?"

"What do you think Julius meant when he said I was a force for change?"

Hat's pom-pom bobbed in a shrug. "Think about it, Julie. You've been trying to get Kaplan to change his recruiting policies since you were hired, and that was only a few weeks ago. You've come into the paranormal world with a whole new perspective. I think he thinks that's what Malcolm needs to become a more well-rounded ruler."

"Poor Malcolm." Julie stifled a yawn. "If there was anything I could do to help him, I would. I don't think he has it easy, even if Julius seems more loving and less old-fashioned than I expected."

"Maybe your alliance with the Noxes can help you affect the changes in OPMA you've been hoping for?" Hat suggested.

Julie pulled her covers up higher and felt a familiar throb at the back of her skull. "Maybe," she mumbled.

Sleep bore her away, and as her eyes closed, Hat gave a small *poof* and transformed into an old-fashioned policeman's cover.

He leaned over and pressed the switch on her bedside lamp with his brim to turn it off.

Hat studied the girl as she slept, her pixie-cut hair mussed on her pillow.

That's my girl, he whispered into her dreams.

Julie hitched her backpack higher on her shoulder. A grin tugged at her lips as she strode across the campus of the Official Para-Military Agency Headquarters.

The green lawns were neatly trimmed, and paranormals of every description were hustling along the pathways even though it was just before eight o'clock in the morning. A knot of elves wearing long white lab coats almost bumped into her, muttering over the reports in their hands.

She skirted two dwarves wearing purple scrubs and a wolf the size of a pony. The wolf had a stethoscope around its neck. When three orcs in blue uniforms with swords on their backs and pistols by their sides strode toward Julie with set jaws and grim eyes, she gave them a wide berth.

Julie looked at the blockish OPMA building. She adjusted Hat on her head to block the bright summer sunshine pouring down on her.

How's your head feeling? Hat asked. *Am I too heavy for you today?*

Nah, you're fine. Julie glanced down at her outfit. She wore gym attire, but her work clothes were in her bag. *Besides, you go so well with those studded jeans when you're in your fedora form.*

Oh, yes. I'm clearly a fashion accessory, Hat snarked, his faint English accent rolling around inside her head.

Julie scoffed as she headed for the door of the gym on one side of the main building. *I'm ready to kick some elf ass today.*

Have you forgotten how many Yeti arses that elf kicked recently? Hat laughed.

Hey, I kicked a few of my own, Julie protested.

Before she reached the door, a looming figure blotted out the sunlight. Julie had to tip her chin up to look her boss in the eye since he was seven feet tall. The weretiger was in his human form, as was usual when he was at work, but that made him no less intimidating. Kaplan's bushy black brows were drawn close together, and his chiseled jaw was set in its usual snarl.

"Meadows," he growled.

Julie took a step back. "Good morning, sir."

"Where do you think you're going?" Kaplan demanded, folding arms with biceps the size of boulders.

"Training, sir." Julie straightened. "You did say I should check back today. It's Monday."

"I said I would check with *you* today." Kaplan's frown deepened. "I think you should still be in bed with that rattled human brain of yours."

"I feel fine, sir. I took it easy over the weekend. Promise." Julie shrugged. "Can I go back to work now?"

Kaplan shook his head and waved a massive hand. "No, you can go to the ER and report to Dr. Olena to be cleared. You can have your mandated physical done, too. It's high time."

There was no use arguing with Kaplan. Julie ripped off a salute. "Whatever you say, sir."

"Was that sarcasm in your tone, Meadows?"

"Whatever you say, sir," Julie repeated, then turned tail and marched to the ER before she could get fired or disemboweled.

You'd better stop by the cafeteria for breakfast if you want to make it through the morning without fainting, Hat pointed out. *Dr. Olena will be taking blood samples, and I think Taylor's had enough of catching you when you fall.*

Don't remind me. Julie groaned inwardly. She changed course for the main building and pulled her phone out of her pocket to text her partner.

Morning! Can't make gym. Sidelined by Kaplan. Gotta go to the ER.

The elf texted back instantly. Julie read it absently as she pushed through the lobby, a vast wood-paneled hall with deep carpets, and headed for the cafeteria.

Are you ok?!!!!!!

Julie laughed. The number of exclamation marks in Taylor's texts was indicative of how freaked out he was.

Fine. Just need to be cleared. See you at work.

Taylor texted back a goat emoji.

"What is with him and the goat?" Julie mumbled as she headed into the cafeteria. The huge room was quiet. There were four long tables running down its length, with a buffet table against one wall. A few people in uniforms sat here and there, with a knot of officers in bright red gathered at the head of one table. Julie grabbed a banana and a piece of toast, munching the toast as she tossed the banana peel in the trash. It would do for breakfast on the go.

Hey, there's your friend, Hat told her.

Taylor? Julie looked up, but there was no sign of the tall, tawny-skinned Aether Elf. At the bottom of one table, a six-foot-tall troll with greenish skin and a long blonde ponytail leaned forward over a cup of coffee, all alone. She wore a white lab coat with IT in a blue circle on the back, and the coffee had a congealed skin on the top. Her shoulders were slumped. Behind her thick glasses, her eyes stared at nothing.

Julie walked over, her smile coming easily. "Hey, Qtana!"

The troll jumped and looked up, eyes wide. She relaxed when she saw Julie. "Oh, hey."

Julie pushed a chair out with one hip and sat. Dr. Olena could wait a few minutes. She'd never seen the peppy IT troll look so down in the mouth. "Are you okay?"

"Yeah!" Qtana pushed her glasses up her nose. "I'm fine. Why?"

"Well, your coffee's gone cold," Julie pointed out. She bit the end off her banana. "And the coffee here is really good, so that's a travesty."

Qtana looked at the mug in her hands as though she were surprised to see it there. "Oh, yeah." She sipped it, then grimaced.

"What's up?" Julie asked.

The troll studied her, and a furrow appeared on her brow above her glasses. Then her shoulders slumped, and she ran her fingers through her ponytail.

"The IT department is sort of chaotic right now." Qtana took another sip of the cold coffee. "Ever since those Yetis escaped."

Julie's stomach tightened at the memory. She considered asking Qtana if she knew whether Leafeyes and Palladius, the good-natured agents who'd been killed during the escape, had any family, but she pushed the thought away. "Is Kaplan putting pressure on you guys to improve the security?"

"Always." Qtana grimaced. "But it's worse than that. IA has been investigating the containment unit breach and the Yeti incursion that followed since it happened."

"IA?" Julie raised her eyebrows. It made sense that the PMA would have an internal affairs branch.

"Yeah. See, the system was hacked." Qtana paused. "I was part of developing that system, Julie. It was airtight. No one should have been able to break into it. We're all under scrutiny now."

"That seems harsh." Julie grimaced. "I bet Qbiit isn't happy about it."

"You know what they say. Shit rolls downhill." Qtana shrugged. "Especially when Qbiit is your boss. Kaplan can be harsh, but I'd rather have him than Qbiit any day."

"I heard him yelling at you over lunch last week." Julie grimaced. "Sounded pretty rough."

"He's a brilliant tech. I've learned a lot from him." Qtana smiled. "He's done a lot for the PMA's security and systems, too."

Ha! Hat snorted. *He'd have done a lot more if he'd allowed me to go on being the recruiting system.*

Still sore about that, are we? Julie chided.

Always. Hat sniffed.

"I think he's just tired and stressed. He's been at work really late all week, trying to figure out what happened to the system." Qtana shrugged again. "I can't blame him for being grumpy."

"Hey, it's no excuse for yelling at you."

"Thanks for saying that." Qtana managed a smile. "I'm sorry for offloading my stress on you. You've had a hard time lately, too. I heard you were hurt in that fight with those Yetis."

"Just a concussion. I'm okay now." Julie patted the troll's arm. "And don't apologize. Everyone needs someone to talk to, and our choices are pretty limited, given the nature of our work."

"That's nice of you." Qtana let out a breath. "Thanks."

"Any time." Julie got up. "I've got to get to the ER to be cleared for duty, but why don't we do lunch sometime?"

Qtana straightened, brightening. "Really? Won't your elf friend mind?"

"Nope." Julie grinned. "I'll be in touch."

I mind! Hat squealed.

Julie ignored him and waved goodbye to Qtana as she hurried out of the cafeteria.

CHAPTER TWO

Dr. Olena's slanting pale-blue eyes creased in a smile when she pulled the curtains aside and found Julie waiting on the hospital bed.

"Well, if it isn't my favorite human patient." The Sylthana Elf brushed a piece of calf-length hair behind her ear.

Julie smirked. "Pretty sure I'm your *only* human patient."

"True, but still." Dr. Olena glanced at her clipboard and set it on the foot of the bed. "How's your head?"

"It was pretty sore on Friday but got much better through the weekend. I didn't take anything for it yesterday, and it didn't bother me." Julie clasped her hands in front of her. "Come on, Doc. Just clear me. I can't stand one more day stuck in my apartment with my mom calling me every ten minutes to preach about the amazing curative properties of aloe vera juice."

"Don't worry. I was planning on it." Dr. Olena laughed. "Any double vision, nausea, or dizziness in the past day or two?"

"None since Friday." Julie paused. "My memory of Thursday night is a little spotty, though."

"That's normal." Dr. Olena shone a pupil light in her eyes. "If your symptoms are gone, you're safe to return to work. Let's get on with the physical."

"Thanks." Julie held out an arm and the elf wrapped a blood pressure cuff around it. Dr. Olena was silent as she inflated the cuff and pressed her stethoscope to the crook of Julie's elbow. "Your blood pressure's a little low. No surprise for someone built like you." Dr. Olena chuckled.

"Thanks, I think?" Julie grinned.

Dr. Olena clipped a pulse oximeter onto Julie's forefinger. "Does your mom live nearby?"

"West Brighton." Julie glanced at the numbers that appeared on the monitor beside the bed. "Too close for comfort sometimes."

Dr. Olena cracked a smile. "My parents still live in Avalon. I hardly ever see them."

Julie frowned. "You must be really busy here in the ER."

"Oh, it's not that. It's just a really long way to travel." The Sylthana Elf shrugged.

Julie blinked at her, trying to put the pieces together. "I've just been to Avalon through the portal in Central Park, so you've lost me."

Dr. Olena unclipped the pulse oximeter and scribbled on her clipboard. "Oh, you were in Avalon Village. My parents live halfway across the kingdom from the village."

"I see." Julie submitted to having her heart and lungs listened to. When Dr. Olena slung her stethoscope around her neck again, she resumed the conversation. "So, Avalon Village is inside Avalon, the paranormal world. Like New York City and New York State."

"Pretty much." Dr. Olena pulled a wheeled tray closer. "How are you with needles?"

"I don't think anyone *likes* needles, but I'm okay." Julie offered an arm.

Dr. Olena made herself comfortable on the edge of the bed

and took Julie's hand, then rested it on her lap. She wrapped a tourniquet around Julie's bicep.

"You miss your parents?" Julie guessed.

Dr. Olena tapped around the crook of Julie's elbow, looking for a vein. "All the time. We were very close when I was growing up. Mom was disappointed when I decided to become a doctor and wanted to work in this ER, but Dad was supportive." She blinked as though she were holding back tears.

Julie put her head to one side. "How do you like life in the human world?"

"A little lonely sometimes." Dr. Olena flashed her a quick smile. "Okay, sharp poke."

Julie managed not to wince as the needle slid into her vein. Dr. Olena started filling blood tubes with quick, steady hands. She tried to remember what it was about Sylthana Elves that had been nagging at the back of her mind since she came to the Para-ER this morning.

Sylthana Elves have continued a political rivalry with the Lunar Fae for centuries, her orb training supplied.

Julie thought about what Hat had said about the Lunar Fae dying out. The Sylthana Elves must be next in line to the Throne. It felt like something she shouldn't bring up to Dr. Olena, but perhaps it was a reason for the loneliness that radiated from the doctor like heat.

After an eye test, a hearing test, and a thing that Julie had to blow into to check her lung capacity, Dr. Olena led her back to the doors of the ER. "I don't know much about humans, but you seem to be a healthy specimen."

Julie laughed. "Thanks."

"You're welcome." Dr. Olena grinned. "Stop by if you have any trouble with your head."

"I'll be okay." Julie hesitated. "Hey, Doc, I was going to have lunch with Qtana from IT sometime. Would you like to join us?"

Dr. Olena perked up. "That sounds great. I'd love to."

"Cool." Julie paused. "Are we done?"

"Oh, yes." Dr. Olena checked her watch. "You'd better hurry if you're going to get to the briefing."

Julie frowned. "What briefing?"

The elevator spat Julie out on the second floor on the first try, for once.

Thanks for your cooperation, Julie mocked it silently as she stepped through the doors.

Aren't we in a cheerful mood? Hat quipped.

Julie adjusted him on her head as she jogged toward the vast auditorium. *I was expecting it to take me to Switzerland or someplace else crazy again.*

There are all kinds of magical locks on the portal to Switzerland now. Don't worry. Hat sighed. *Why do you care so much about this briefing? Kaplan would have ordered you to be there if he wanted you there.*

That's my point! Julie snorted. *Taylor and I have been in the middle of this Yeti thing from the start, so why wasn't I asked to attend the briefing?*

Speciesism? Hat snarked.

Julie growled. *Don't get me started on that crap.* She reached the vast doors, which were open just enough for her to squeeze inside.

The auditorium was much bigger than she'd expected. Hundreds of seats arced toward a well-lit stage at the back of the room. The seats were upholstered in plush red velvet, and the hardwood floor of the stage gleamed under the spotlights. In the middle of the stage, standing by a small lectern, was Kaplan. The weretiger leaned over his notes, and on the massive screen that stretched across the wall behind him, Julie could see his full eyebrows touching as he frowned.

Julie glanced left and right, looking for an open seat. The spaces were mostly filled by paranormals in blue, red, purple, and white, but there was no sign of green.

Seriously? she hissed. *The IT department is here, but not a single recruiter.*

Guess you're lower down the ladder than you expected, Hat retorted.

Julie scoffed at him and spotted a familiar face in the crowd. It was youthful and handsome, and a wing of blond hair fell over a stern forehead. She waved and the young werewolf spun in his seat, waving back with huge enthusiasm and gesturing at the empty seat beside his.

Julie chuckled as she hurried over. "Hey, Isaiah! Nice to see you here."

"It's nice to see you, too." Isaiah beamed. "Look, guys, it's that chick who strung us up in the trees in Montana!"

"Hey!" the other five werewolves chorused, waving at her.

"How's the elf dude?" the biggest and brashest of the lot asked. Chester was his name, Julie remembered.

"He's good." Julie sat beside Isaiah. "How's Bootcamp treating you?"

"We got our first orb training over the weekend." Isaiah's eyes widened. "That shit is crazy."

"I'm glad you're enjoying yourselves." Julie laughed. "I think you're going to like working in the PMA."

Isaiah shrugged. "It beats chasing an angry centaur's horses for kicks. So far, anyway."

Julie smiled as the auditorium's lights dimmed and silence fell. *Another set of happy recruits.*

Hat snorted. *Not to blow your own trumpet or anything.*

"Good morning." Kaplan's voice reverberated around the auditorium, though Julie couldn't see a mic on the lectern.

Julie glanced around, looking for speakers. Instead, she

spotted a tiny window above her head in the back of the room and got a glimpse of greenish skin through the gap. IT trolls.

"There have been concerning developments in the Yeti issue," Kaplan went on. "We will begin..." He paused, nose twitching, then his burning amber eyes flicked to where Julie sat next to the Weres. She saw his eyes narrow, and she expected to be dragged kicking and screaming from the room. Instead, Kaplan continued his briefing. "We will begin by recapping the events of the past few weeks."

The captain turned his back to the lectern and looked at the screen. His face disappeared, replaced by a PowerPoint presentation.

PowerPoint? Hat sneered. *You must be joking.*

Shhh! I'm trying to pay attention. Julie squinted at the timeline on the screen.

"In April, Malcolm Nox, the son of Julius Nox and the heir to the vampire throne, was attacked and mugged by a large male Yeti." Kaplan used a laser pointer to indicate a photograph of the nasty wounds the Yeti had inflicted on Malcolm's shoulder. "At that time, the Yeti was acting alone. It took Nox's wallet, watch, and mobile phone. That behavior makes no sense since Yetis are not known to have personal possessions or use currency."

Julie leaned back in her seat, waiting for the orb to help her. Her training filtered into her consciousness.

Yetis are a simple species who, although they exhibit high intelligence, appear to have little interest in currency, politics, conflict, science, or ownership. Their monarchy has been handed down peaceably through the same family throughout history. They use their considerable creative abilities to craft intricate stories and the most complex music in the paranormal world.

She frowned, reaching up to rub the still-tender spot on the back of her head where a Yeti had flung her into the wall of a sewer tunnel on Thursday night. Peaceful musicians and storytellers?

Kaplan went on, echoing her thoughts, "The Yetis' behavior has been inconsistent with their nature since the attack on Mr. Nox. Muggings have been reported all over the city in the past weeks, during which paranormals have been violently attacked even after complying with the Yetis' demands.

"To make matters worse, the first few mugging victims reported a lone attacker. In the past two weeks, however, several muggings have taken place in which two or three Yetis have attacked the victim."

A murmur ran through the crowd. Isaiah glanced at the other werewolves and then at Julie, his eyebrows raised.

"Eight days ago, a Yeti attacked Aether Elf prince Taylor Woodskin in a parking garage in Manhattan." Kaplan continued as the crowd's murmurs grew louder. "The prince was unharmed, and the Yeti was arrested and brought to the OPMA for interrogation. Before this could happen, however, the Yeti escaped. The computer system controlling the doors in the containment unit was hacked."

Kaplan's eyes narrowed as they rested on the window above Julie's head. "Days later, they returned to the OPMA through a portal. They appeared to have a mission to push deeper into the building, perhaps to the Shrine of Previous Technology and Magic, but six courageous individuals, four scientists and two agents, confronted them in the hall and held them off until reinforcements could arrive. Five were killed in the fight. The sixth died less than an hour later.

"Make no mistake." Kaplan pointed at the pictures on the screen. "They were all murdered."

The auditorium was deathly silent. For once, Kaplan's voice held no hint of a snarl as he pulled up photographs of six paranormals. Julie stared at the pictures of Agents Leafeyes and Palladius, a scruffy elf with shaggy hair and a dapper dwarf in a neat suit. She swallowed around the lump in her throat.

Hat gave her head a gentle squeeze. *Julie, you barely knew them.*

Does that matter? Julie swallowed again. *They were kind to me. They were* people, *Hat. Real people with families and lives, and they're gone because of this. They died trying to protect the PMA.* Her hands bunched into fists at her sides.

Kaplan read the names of the fallen one by one. "Agent Antimony Palladius and Agent Cooper Leafeyes." He cleared his throat, then turned to face the audience again. "Look at these faces. Remember them. Remember their names. These paranormals died serving and protecting the Eternity Throne and the good of Avalon and all paranormals. What's more, they died violently, senselessly, and far too young. I will not lose any more people."

Julie squeezed her fists tightly. She had thought of grabbing coffee with Leafeyes and Palladius, hearing war stories and listening to their wisdom. She wondered if they had kids. Kids who had heard the same words she had once heard, words that had broken her world. "I'm sorry, honey. Dad's not coming home."

"Look at these pictures, people. Look at them *again!*" Kaplan thundered. "Let them be your reason for finding the source of the Yeti incursion and putting a stop to it once and for all."

Beside Julie, the Weres were silent, their eyes fixed on the screen. A muscle jumped in Isaiah's jaw as he clenched it.

"Another violent incident occurred Thursday night." Kaplan switched to the next slide, showing pictures of the sewer tunnel where the fight had taken place. Julie tried not to look at the blurred images of the dead Yetis lying in the tunnel. She knew Taylor and Malcolm had fought in self-defense, but the bodies made her gut twist.

"Malcolm Nox and two OPMA recruiters spotted a lone Yeti moving through the streets of Bay Ridge." Kaplan aimed the laser pointer at a map at the bottom of the screen. "They tracked it to an abandoned garment factory in Industry City, Bush Terminal, and followed it through a maintenance door into the sewer system below. Without waiting for backup from actual PMA agents, I might add." Kaplan looked over his shoulder, and his eyes found Julie.

She let out a breath. At least he didn't mention her by name.

"Alarmingly, when the imbecilic trio reached this point in the sewer system, they were attacked by not two or three Yetis, but twenty or more." Kaplan indicated another spot on the map. "Enough that Prince Taylor and Mr. Nox were wounded in the fight, as well as their companion, recruiter Julie Meadows." Her photo popped up on the screen.

Hundreds of eyes turned to her. She wished a portal would appear under her chair and whisk her off to somewhere else. A dragon's keep, perhaps. Anywhere that wasn't here.

Isaiah leaned in close. "Cool!" he whispered. "You fought those Yetis?"

"Shhh!" his friends chorused.

Kaplan turned to the crowd. "When PMA agents arrived on the scene, the Yetis fled. After forensic reports came back, it was clear that the Yetis had escaped through a portal."

Protests burst from the crowd.

"That's impossible!" an orc cried.

"How?" squealed a fae.

Hat, that can't be right. Julie stared at her hands. *On Thursday, you guys told me that only the PMA and other agencies connected to the Eternity Throne had the tech to make portals.*

It's true. Hat's tone was grim. *Someone from the PMA was behind that.*

Kaplan sharply raised a hand, and the crowd hushed.

"You heard correctly," he snarled, his growl rumbling in Julie's bones. "Someone inside the OPMA is responsible for the attack on HQ and the deaths of these agents." His voice dropped another octave. "Someone inside this room."

Julie's heart thudded as she glanced left and right. There were hardly any familiar faces in the crowd, but her eyes dwelled on the people she did know. Dr. Olena. Qtana. The young werewolves.

"No one will leave this auditorium until they are cleared by IA." Kaplan set down his laser pointer and swept the room with a glare.

Julie clutched the sides of her seat. *Who would do this?* she ranted inwardly. *How could someone who knew Leafeyes and Palladius and those scientists kill them?*

It's okay. Just sit tight, Hat told her, *and wait your turn to see IA.*

Julie's stomach clenched. *That doesn't sound good.*

Hat chuckled. *I'm pretty sure it's not what you think.*

"Rest assured," Kaplan snarled, his voice echoing around the auditorium, "that when I find the culprit, their exit interview will conclude with a call to the undertaker."

He stormed off the stage, his three hundred pounds thundering over the boards, and Isaiah turned to Julie. "He's joking, right?"

Julie shrugged. "I don't think so."

An officer in a red uniform barked, "You! Come here!" at the young Weres, and they scurried toward him. Julie was left alone in an ever-widening circle as people gathered in little knots, waiting to be interviewed. The knots all seemed to be the same colors, soldiers and agents in little blue groups, scientists in white, and officers in red. Julie was beginning to think she should have worn her green uniform.

She swung her legs to shake some of the tightness out of them and tilted her head from side to side.

Is your head okay? Hat asked.

Julie stopped. *Yeah, my neck just feels stiff.*

Stop that. You're making me seasick.

Julie didn't smile at his quip. She stared at her hands, which were knotted in her lap, as the minutes ticked past and one person at a time traipsed through the doors of the auditorium.

Her phone buzzed at a quarter past nine.

Where are you????

Four question marks. Not a good sign. Julie picked up her phone and texted Taylor back.

In the auditorium.

What? You're at the briefing? Why????

Julie sighed. **Tell you later. Gotta talk to IA before I can come to the office.**

Seriously?????

Five question marks now. Taylor was going to have a coronary if he went on like this. **Everything is okay,** Julie responded. **Start looking for another recruit while you wait.**

Taylor sent the shrug emoji. **Okay.**

She began to wish she was holed up in her comfy office, working on that report Kaplan had asked for about how to improve recruitment numbers and bantering with Taylor. She even missed the ugly Renaissance-era portrait of the mermaid with strategically placed hair that hung on their wall for no apparent reason.

The circle around her was growing wider. *Feeling a bit unpopular,* she thought.

It's because you're the only recruiter, Hat told her.

Julie glanced at the screen again, remembering her picture on it. *Sure it is.*

CHAPTER THREE

Almost an hour had gone by. Julie was starting to wonder if she could risk running the gauntlet to the auditorium bathrooms on the other side of the room when a heavy weight flopped on the chair beside hers. "So, is it true? Are you an imbecile?"

Julie whipped around, laughing. Isaiah was lolling on the chair beside hers, and the other Weres had piled into place beside him.

"An imbecile?" Julie echoed.

"Kaplan called you, Mr. Nox, and Prince Taylor the 'imbecilic trio.'" The smallest Were, a dark-haired boy with a quick smile, shrugged.

"What Noah said." Chester jerked a thumb at his friend.

Julie couldn't help grinning. There was something different about these Weres. They weren't fighting among themselves, even in this situation.

Less like a frat on Spring Break, Hat suggested.

Julie stifled a snicker. "What we did *was* pretty stupid," she conceded.

"Were there really twenty Yetis?" Noah asked.

"Felt like more at the time." Julie laughed. "So, how's Bootcamp? Only one of you answered me."

"Martial arts is *lit!*" Chester whooped.

Another Were, a stocky guy with intelligent eyes, scoffed. "Yeah, not so much for anyone weighing less than two hundred and fifty pounds."

"Aw, don't worry, Teddy. You'll get the hang of it." Isaiah prodded him in the chest.

"Our teacher was kind of scary," Noah chipped in. "Really intense."

"I thought Blake was going to piss himself." Chester chortled.

"Wait." Julie laughed and held up her hands. "There are too many of you. Let me be sure I've got your names straight. Isaiah, Chester, Noah." She pointed at each in turn. "Teddy, Blake, and…"

"Austin." The last Were grinned.

"Say, ma'am." Blake, who was well over six feet and composed mostly of knees and elbows, fixed Julie with big, soulful eyes. "I wanted to say thank you for recruiting us. We caused a lot of trouble back home, and the truth is, we just needed a sense of direction. Things are much better here."

"Yeah, Blake's right." Isaiah nodded. "Our lives are a lot better here. We're looking forward to becoming real soldiers at the PMA."

Julie beamed. "Make sure you become good ones, guys. It looks like we're going to need you."

"Yes, ma'am." Blake nodded, his face serious.

The auditorium door swung open. "Meadows, Julie," a female called.

"That's me." Julie got up and headed for the doors, wiping sweat from her palms as she walked.

A disenchanted dwarf in a staid brown uniform was waiting at the door. She squinted at Julie, then at the list in her hand. "ID," she growled.

Julie held out her ID tag, and the dwarf briefly glanced at it. "Fine. Follow me."

The dwarf led her down a short, silent hallway and into a room only slightly smaller than the auditorium. It echoed with emptiness. When the dwarf slammed the door behind Julie, she jumped when the *slam* reverberated through the room. The room's flat floor stretched in front of her, featureless but for the stone platform that rose from the center. The platform was large, solid, and pyramid-shaped, with a flat square top and steps cut into its sides.

That's them, Hat hissed. *That's IA.*

Julie blinked. On top of the platform sat three…*cats?* Strange-looking felines but normal nonetheless, each the size and shape of her landlady's cat. The only major difference was that instead of being fluffy, these had no fur. Their skin was as bare as hers, and it wrinkled in folds at their hips and bellies as they sat on the platform, watching her in silence with unblinking green eyes.

They're Sphynx cats, Julie told Hat. *Bred in Canada during the 1960s.*

Ha! Hat snorted. *That's what* you *think.*

Before Julie could ask him what he meant, one of the Sphynxes blinked. "You must be the human."

Hat's crown sagged with relief when the Sphynx uttered the words. He got to his feet, his naked tail rising into the air as he stepped closer to the edge of the platform. "Come closer, little human," the cat ordered.

One of the other Sphynxes watched, creepily unmoving. The other lay down and began licking her paws.

Okay, Hat grumbled. *You're overdoing it now.*

The Sphynx huffed at Hat. *Would you rather I told her?*

No! Hat shouted. *You know there would be consequences. Dire consequences.*

The Sphynx cast him a lazy glance. The slit pupils narrowed as he lay down at the edge of the platform, his paws draped elegantly in front of him. *You have already threatened me in your most dangerous form. I'm terribly frightened.* His tail lashed over his haunches. *But she should know.*

Not from you! Hat protested.

The Sphynx sighed and turned his attention to Julie. "I've heard about you, *human*," he purred, glancing at Hat again. "It seems you have a nose for trouble."

"Not intentionally, sir." Julie cocked her head to one side, almost losing Hat as she studied the IA agent. "Are you really a cat?"

"I'm a Sphynx." The cat yawned, showing off sharp white teeth. "You already knew that, didn't you? The only difference is that I'm not from Canada. The Canadian breed was based on my descendants, who are far less magical than we are."

"*Far* less magical." Another Sphynx scoffed.

The first Sphynx nodded. "We come from Ancient Egypt. They used to worship us there, you know. Not terribly different from what people do these days." He blinked.

You're wasting time, Hat grumbled. *You knew she was innocent when she walked into the room.*

Might as well keep up appearances. The Sphynx jumped off the platform in a lithe movement and sat on his haunches in front of Julie, looking up at her. "You have a question, human. Speak."

"If you're so ancient and magical, why are you working in Internal Affairs for the PMA?" Julie asked. "It's not a very glamorous gig after being worshiped."

"It's not glamorous, but it's also not boring." The Sphynx wrapped his tail around his paws. "Do you know how boring life becomes when you're an arbiter of truth who's been alive for thousands of years? This gives us something to do."

"An arbiter of truth." Julie folded her arms. "So, you can sense lies."

"Exactly." The Sphynx methodically began to lick his paws.

Julie watched. Hat watched. The Sphynx moved on from his paws to his shoulders, twisting and sticking his tail out for balance so that he could reach the itchy spots. Hat struggled to stifle a sigh of irritation.

Julie spoke after two minutes. "Uh, can I go now?"

The Sphynx paused long enough to say, "Did I say you could go?" and started on his upper back.

Hat? Julie asked. *What am I supposed to do?*

You'll just have to roll with it. Sorry, Hat offered.

Can't you get them to cut it out and let me go? You're also ancient and magical, right? Julie pleaded.

I know better than to match wits with a Sphynx, Hat admitted.

At this, the Sphynx stopped washing and looked at Hat, a purr rumbling in his chest. Hat stifled a sigh. He wasn't going to hear the end of this.

"Very well, human. Your interview shall now begin." The Sphynx fixed his golden eyes on Julie's face. "Where were you on the night the Yetis broke through and killed four scientists and Agents Palladius and Leafeyes?"

Julie flinched at the names of the two agents. "Home," she mumbled. She was about to say her landlady Lillie could confirm that but stopped. *I can't put Lillie in danger.*

Relax. They can sense if you're lying, remember? Hat grumbled.

The Sphynx cocked his head to one side. "What were you doing at home?"

"What was I—" Julie paused. "Uh, well, I made dinner and read a few chapters of Tolstoy's *Anna Karenina*, then I went to sleep."

"Ah, Tolstoy. Do you normally read such viscerally boring work?" the Sphynx asked.

Julie bridled. "Hey, *The Story of Sinuhe* wasn't much better. I happen to like Tolstoy."

"Interesting," the Sphynx purred, "considering that when you were twelve years old, you told your mother you would rather shove your copy of *War and Peace* down her throat than read it."

Julie had been replaying that memory in her mind. She sputtered, "That was different! I was twelve!"

"You were also convinced that you wanted to be a doctor when you grew up." The Sphynx hesitated. "I'm sorry about your father."

Heat radiated from Julie's cheeks to Hat's brim. "What does that have to do with your investigation?"

"Do you think your problems with authority stem from the poor math teacher you had in second grade?" the Sphynx asked.

"I don't have problems with—" Julie stopped.

The Sphynx chuckled. "Tricky, isn't it?"

"Why can't you just pose riddles like a normal Sphynx?" Julie grumbled.

"Because I know you know most of the answers, you clever little human." The Sphynx got to his feet and stretched luxuriously, his tail curling up over his back. "Tell me a little more about yourself, Miss Meadows. How are you always in the middle of whatever Yeti activity is going on?"

You know very well why, Hat hissed.

The Sphynx smirked at him. *You're the one who wants me to finish conducting this interview for appearance's sake.*

"I don't know. I don't know why that Yeti attacked Taylor in the parking garage. I felt like I had to help Malcolm Nox, and that's why I went into the sewers with him." Julie gritted her teeth. "I stand by that decision."

"Admirable, I'm sure." The Sphynx rolled onto his back, playfully patting the air. "Do you have any catnip?"

"Catnip?" Julie frowned. "That's illegal in the para world."

"Never mind. Tell me a little more about yourself, Miss Meadows. What do you do for fun?"

"Read, I guess." Julie shrugged. "Like I said. *Anna Karenina*."

"Yes, yes." The Sphynx rolled to his feet. "Do you think that's why you're nineteen years old and have never had a steady boyfriend?"

Julie flushed. "I don't have time for that."

"Not even when you were unemployed and meeting dodgy strangers from dating apps?" the Sphynx inquired. "You should have avoided Sam from the start, by the way. There were plenty of red flags on his profile."

"Don't see how this has anything to do with your investigation," Julie growled.

The Sphynx flicked his ears. "I'm just hoping you'll give me more of a sense of who you really are, Miss Meadows."

Careful, Hat growled at the Sphynx.

Julie put her hands on her hips. Hat groaned. That was never a good sign. "Why should I? You're reading my mind," the human sassed.

The Sphynx purred. "Oh, *very* good. There's no point in denying it. I know you already know."

"Then what am I still doing here?" Julie tipped her chin up. Hat groaned again. Even worse. "You know I'm innocent if you can read my mind."

The Sphynx chuckled. "Miss Meadows, I can't read your subconscious, can I? All I know is what's going through your thoughts at this moment. That's handy for the purposes of an internal affairs investigation. Most people think about their guilt or innocence the moment they walk into a room."

"You know I'm innocent."

"Oh, yes." The Sphynx padded over to her and arched against her shins, purring ecstatically. "You may tickle me under the chin now. I know you've wanted to since you came into the room."

"Fine," Julie mumbled. She bent down and gave the Sphynx a

gentle rub under the chin, which caused him to purr like an engine. He finally stalked away with his tail in the air.

"You may go now," he called over his shoulder.

"Thanks, I guess." Julie's shoulders sagged with relief.

She turned to go, and the Sphynx called, "Miss Meadows?"

"Yeah?" Julie looked back.

The Sphynx was back on top of the platform, paws crossed over the edge. He blinked. "Trouble will continue to find you. Expect it."

She stared at him, decided against asking why, and headed for the door.

What was that? Hat hissed at the Sphynx.

You'll have to tell her sometime, you know, the Sphynx added. *Next!*

The dwarf led Julie to the room containing the elevator.

The recruiter kneaded her aching temples. "That was some crazy shit. I feel like I've just gone through the mental equivalent of a spin cycle in the washing machine."

"Trust me. They went easy on you," Hat grumbled.

The elevator doors opened as Julie reached it, and a willowy young elf in a green uniform stepped out. His chocolate-brown eyes widened when he saw Julie. "You've got to come with me. Now."

"Good morning to you too, Taylor," Julie told her partner. "It's nice to see you, and my head feels much better, thanks."

"*Now,* Julie." Taylor grabbed her arm and towed her into the elevator.

Julie started to protest, but the look on his face stopped her. "Taylor, what's going on?"

"Julius Nox just came to our office." The elf swallowed audibly. "Malcolm's missing."

Kaplan sat behind his huge desk, fingers steepled in front of him. Over his shoulder, Julie could see the campus through a floor-to-ceiling window. She resisted the urge to stare outside as if Malcolm would materialize out on the lawn and march toward the lab with its serious-looking scientists or loll on the grass with the recruits on break.

She dragged her eyes back to the captain. She hadn't seen Kaplan look pale before. His brows were disheveled, and it was easy to see why when he passed a massive hand over his face and turned his attention to Julius Nox. The vampire sat in one of the chairs in front of the desk. His usually smooth ponytail was a mess this morning, and he had wisps of hair hanging around his face. Julie and Taylor stood next to him.

"All right, Julius." Kaplan returned his hands to the desk. "Tell them what you told me."

The lines around the vampire's face had deepened in the few hours since Julie had last seen him. He took a shaky breath. "I don't know how long he's been gone, but I can't find him anywhere."

Julie wanted to put a hand on Julius' shoulder, but she wasn't sure she was allowed to in front of Kaplan. Wasn't there something about touching royalty? "Didn't he go home with you on Thursday night, Sire?"

"He did." Julius shook his head. "Everything was fine over the weekend. He spent most of his time in his suite, playing that stupid video game with his online friends." The vampire groaned. "I should have paid more attention. I should have talked to him, but I thought he was sulking after I reprimanded him about his actions."

"There's no time for blame now, Julius," Kaplan interjected. His voice was lower than usual. "We need to find him."

"Of course, Jack." Julius took a shaky breath. "This morning, Malcolm didn't come down for dinner."

Oh, yeah. Vampires are nocturnal, Julie reminded herself.

"It's not unusual. Sometimes he has dinner sent to his suite when he's deep in a game. Occasionally he plays video games all day and sleeps all night, although I'm sure it's not good for his sleep schedule."

Julius frowned. "I was concerned, so I went up and knocked on his door. He ignored me. I could hear that stupid game, so I assumed he couldn't hear me or wasn't interested in talking, so I left."

Julie thought about what Julius had said on Friday night about allowing Malcolm his freedom.

"I woke up in the morning, realized Malcolm wasn't done with this Yeti, and couldn't get back to sleep. I went up to check if he was okay, but he was gone." Julius spread his elegant hands. "Just gone."

He's taking it hard, Hat murmured.

Looks like King Daddy Vampire has more feelings than I gave him credit for, Julie agreed.

"Was there any sign of a struggle?" Kaplan asked. "Any Yeti smell?"

"Kidnapping would be very strange Yeti behavior," Hat interjected.

Kaplan gave him a furious glance that seemed to singe Julie's eyebrows. "I didn't ask for your opinion, DUMB LE Dork. *All* of this has been very strange Yeti behavior."

"No, everything was tidy and orderly, and the window was wide open." Julius hung his head. "Malcolm departed of his own accord, but he left his phone behind. I have no way of getting in touch with him. To make matters worse, I've lost his scent. I tracked it a couple of blocks from our home before it disappeared."

Kaplan let out a low growl.

"Sire, if I may." Julie stepped forward, hands behind her back. "I don't understand why Malcolm would do this. All he wants is to prove himself to you. He knows you disapprove of what he did, so..." She glanced at Kaplan, but the weretiger made no move to stop her. "Is it possible that someone took him and staged it to look like he left of his own accord? I mean, it doesn't make sense for Malcolm to just go."

"Meadows," Kaplan growled.

"No, it's all right, Jack." Julius held up a hand. "You're right, Miss Meadows. It doesn't make sense, but Malcolm is not thinking reasonably. Do you know what the Quickening is?"

Julie's orb training leaped to the forefront of her mind, but she pushed it aside. Now wasn't the time to stand around glassy-eyed, listening to the voice in her head. "No, Sire. I'm not familiar."

"We don't have time for a lecture on vampire biology," Kaplan grumbled.

Julius ignored him, a power move if Julie had ever seen one. "When vampires are not yet of age, their powers are, shall we say, muted," he explained. "Young vampires have greater strength and speed and better senses than humans do, as well as some ability to mesmerize, but they have far less power than adult vampires."

Julie mulled that over. "It makes sense, Sire. Who needs a bunch of baby vamps running around mind-controlling anyone who looks like they'd make a tasty snack?"

Julius' lips quirked. "Interestingly put, but yes. Malcolm is on the cusp of coming of age. He's about to come fully into his vampire powers. It is a turbulent time for any vampire, and more so for an especially powerful young Nox."

"'Turbulent?'" Julie prompted.

"The Quickening can produce a variety of signs. Surges of emotion, or reckless and unreasonable behavior, are some of them."

Yeah, puberty will do that to you. Julie kept that thought to herself. "Sounds like him lately."

"There's more." Julius winced. "Random exhibits of vampire abilities is another. And a third? Well, a third is fixation. Intense, irresistible obsession with someone or something, even when it doesn't make sense." He sighed heavily, staring at the surface of Kaplan's desk as though it contained the answers.

Julie spoke slowly. "You think he's fixated on this Yeti, Sire?"

Julius' shoulders slumped. "I thought Cassidy was his fixation. It didn't make sense for him to be attracted to the girl but marry someone he didn't love for the good of the family. I-I thought Malcolm hadn't reached that level of maturity yet."

"We'll find him, Julius." Kaplan leaned over his desk and gripped the vampire's forearm. "I know we will."

"If I'd only realized the Yeti was a fixation in time!" Julius lapsed into silence.

I think I know what Cassidy's fixation is, Julie told Hat. *It might be the explanation for her batshit-craziness.*

I think she's just a bitch, Hat admitted.

Yeah, but maybe she's fixated on Malcolm, and it's bringing it out. Anyway, this explains a lot about both Cassidy and Malcolm. Julie turned to Julius, keeping her tone low. "Sire, I'm really sorry to hear about Malcolm's disappearance, but I'm not sure what I can do to help. I haven't heard from him since Friday."

"You two are going to do plenty." Kaplan leaned forward, smirking.

Julie snuck a glance at Taylor, who was gazing at the captain in alarm.

"Until IA has finished interviewing every person in that auditorium, and I'm *certain* I've found the traitor who killed my people and gave portal magic to the Yetis or to whatever is causing the Yetis to act this way..." Kaplan's words ended in a growl, and he paused to compose himself. "Until then, I'm limited in who I can send to look for Malcolm."

"Sir, you can't mean you want to send *us*!" Taylor gasped.

Kaplan's smile widened.

"Sir, we're just recruiters!" the elf protested.

"You're some of my best, Woodskin." Kaplan slammed a hand on the desk with a force that made the floor judder. "That means that you're good at tracking paranormals."

Julie turned to Julius. "Don't you want agents on this, Sire?"

Julius produced a slight smile. "I would think you would want to be in the middle of this, Miss Meadows. You seem to like being in the center of the chaos."

With an effort, Julie stifled a grin. "No comment, Sire. I just want what's best for Malcolm."

"As do we all." Kaplan sat back in his chair. "I would send an army of agents if I could, but right now, my very best are tracking the Yetis, which, by default, will help us find Malcolm. In the meantime, I need someone to look for *him*. Someone I trust."

Julie was unable to look away from Kaplan's burning amber eyes. *Was that a compliment?*

You are one of the few who has received one from Jack Kaplan, Hat grouched.

"Besides." Kaplan smirked. "Malcolm has bonded with you two for whatever reason, so he's much less likely to kill you on sight in the middle of a Quickening rage."

"'*Less likely?*'" Taylor groaned. "All due respect, Captain, that's not comforting."

Julie glanced at Julius again. The vampire seemed to have shrunk several inches overnight. He huddled in his chair, and his skin had turned white, though he had been almost translucent before. Malcolm's boyish grin filled her mind, and the way he'd stood over her and Taylor in that sewer, ready to fight to the death.

She had other plans for Malcolm Nox, whether he knew it or not—assuming this Quickening didn't land him in a situation he couldn't get out of.

"Sir, I want to help." Julie turned to Kaplan. "I'll do whatever you want me to do to find him."

"Me too." Taylor stepped forward. "I'm all in, sir."

Kaplan's lips twitched. Out of the corner of her eye, Julie saw Julius' shoulders sag.

"Very well." Kaplan grabbed a piece of paper from his desk drawer and signed it with a flourish, his giant hand engulfing the pen. "Here. You're both authorized to requisition whatever you think will help you succeed."

Julie hid her smirk of excitement. "Thank you, sir." She took the document.

"Dismissed." Kaplan turned to Julius.

Julie and Taylor hurried out into the bullpen and headed for their office on one side. Taylor glanced at her. "What did we just agree to do?"

"Kaplan said we could requisition whatever we needed." Julie grinned. "Do you think he meant it?"

Hat chuckled. "It's time to visit the Shrine of Previous Technology and Magic."

"Oh, yeah." Julie grinned.

Taylor groaned.

CHAPTER FOUR

Julie's toes curled inside her boots as the elevator whisked them down to the twelfth floor below ground, or the floor designated as such. They had taken a brief and regrettable detour along the way when the elevator doors had opened into a dungeon containing an angry manticore, but it wasn't the manticore that had Julie sweating.

"Let's hope we're actually going to the SPTM," Taylor grumbled, mopping a speck of manticore venom from his shoulder with a baby wipe given to him by the manticore's apologetic keeper. The man had said, "He's not usually like this. He's teething."

"Yeah, well." Julie grimaced. "Do you think those guards are going to hold a grudge against me for last time?"

"You mean when you stole me out and almost cost them their jobs?" Hat inquired helpfully. "Then got them into even more trouble when you got off scot-free, *and* you were allowed to keep me?"

Julie winced. "Yeah, that time."

"I'm sure they're over it." Taylor patted her shoulder. "Aether Elves are a forgiving people."

"Uh-huh. Sure they are," Julie muttered.

The elevator doors slid open to reveal a small space with two massive doors guarded by a familiar pair of burly elves. Julie cringed inwardly as both elves' eyes swept to her, and the shorter of the two raised a finger and barked, "Hey! It's her!"

"You got some cheek, coming down here," grumbled the other. "With *that* on your head, too."

"I can hear you!" Hat protested.

"Look, guys, I'm really sorry." Julie spread her hands. "I didn't mean to get you into trouble when I took DUMB LE Dork. I was really desperate. To be honest, I thought that I was going to be killed if I didn't get a recruit within the week."

"Killed?" The short guard scoffed. "By who?"

"By *whom*," Hat mumbled.

"Kaplan." Julie raised her hands.

"*Why?*" The taller guard snorted.

Julie glanced at Taylor, who had gone the shade of gray he did when he was embarrassed. "Let's not get into it now. The thing is, I'm sorry, and this time I won't get you into any trouble." She held out the requisition form Kaplan had signed. "Everything's aboveboard."

The taller guard took the piece of paper and raised both eyebrows. "Kaplan's letting you take anything you want from the SPTM?"

"That's right." Taylor stepped forward. "Can we go inside now?"

The two guards eyed them, then the taller one sighed and gave Julie the document back. "Anything to declare?"

For a few precarious seconds, they stared at one another. The shorter guard ran a hand down his muscular body and batted his eyelashes. "*All* this!"

Laughter echoed inside the little room. The door slid open, and Taylor and Julie stepped into the Warehouse. Its enormity took Julie's breath away, and she froze for a moment, gazing at the endless shelves of priceless dusty relics.

"Some of these are rubbish." Hat was reading her mind again. "*I* am priceless beyond measure."

"Sure." Julie stepped forward. "I dibs Merlin's wand."

"Merlin's wand?" Taylor squawked. "Need I remind you that Merlin was one of the most powerful warlocks ever to walk this earth, and he forged that wand from moonlight and water crystals at the zenith of a midsummer night at the full moon in the center of Stonehenge while druids chanted all around him? The stars themselves wept at its beauty."

"Still a stuck-up old arse," Hat grumbled.

"You memorize that in grade school?" Julie inquired.

Taylor snorted as he went into the Warehouse. "Maybe. What I'm trying to say is if you touch Merlin's wand, it might kill you. I know better than to touch it, and I have magic."

"Gee, thanks." Julie paused. "Oooh, look, the dragon scale. Does it do magic stuff?"

"Yes, it's a solid at six hundred degrees," Taylor called over his shoulder, poking around on a shelf.

Julie withdrew her finger, having come precariously close to touching the shiny gold scale. "The air around it doesn't feel hot."

"Dragon magic," Hat muttered. "Creepy shit."

"You're creepy shit too, FYI." Julie turned. "Come on, Hat. You've got to have some ideas of things I could use."

There was a crash as Taylor rummaged through a pile of sheathed swords. Something rolled out of the pile and skidded to the floor a few feet from Julie—a huge round shield made of beaten bronze. When Julie picked it up, she was startled by its weight. It almost covered her body.

"This is cool." She hefted the shield. "I never thought I'd see an ancient Greek aspis in real life."

"An ancient Greek what?" Taylor straightened as he pulled out a long white scabbard with a hilt that gleamed like ivory protruding from it.

"An aspis. The shield." Julie held it up.

"That's not just a shield." Taylor chuckled. "That's the shield Perseus used to kill Medusa."

"What?" Julie gaped at it. "Are you serious?"

Hat scoffed. "More balls than brains, Perseus, considering how long it took him to figure that trick out. Daddy issues, too. I mean, why else would you want to murder a Gorgon?"

Julie hesitated. "Well, the way I heard the story, Medusa was doing some murdering of her own."

Taylor rolled his eyes. "That's a very patriarchal version of the narrative. Gorgons are beautiful, peaceful ladies. Medusa was no different."

Taylor set the ivory-hilted sword to one side and went on rummaging through the pile. Julie laid down the shield with distaste and went over to a nearby shelf to admire a dagger resting on a stand. Its hilt was wrought of iron and gold, and the long steel blade had something mixed in with it. It shimmered improbably in the dull gloom of the Warehouse.

"This looks interesting." Julie carefully lifted the dagger and swished it a couple of times. Its blade sang hungrily.

"Careful with that. It's alicorn." Taylor had given up on the swords and was now rummaging through a barrel filled with staffs.

"Alicorn?" Julie asked.

"Unicorn horn." Taylor picked up a wooden staff with a glowing green jewel at one end. "It's the strongest substance in the paranormal world and can be sharpened to an incredible edge, but it's cursed."

"Cursed?" Julie gingerly replaced the dagger.

"What do *you* think would happen if you killed something as wild and beautiful as a unicorn to make a weapon from its horn?"

Hat grunted. "They're bloody dangerous, too. Only the most powerful paras can defeat one."

A pricking shudder went down her spine at the thought. She backed away from the dagger and watched Taylor spin the staff this way and that. He pointed it at the floor, and a blast of blue fire spread around him in a flickering pool, the air shimmering with heat above it.

"Dude!" Julie stared. "That was cool."

Taylor flicked the staff again, and the fire disappeared. "Not really." He grinned sheepishly. "It was pre-charged with the blue fire spell. That wasn't my magic. I can't do much other than make things levitate. I can do shadows too, but they're not very good."

"Do Aether Elves normally have more magic than that?" Julie asked. She went over to the staff barrel and poked through it.

"I *have* more magic. I was just a lazy student," Taylor admitted.

Julie spotted a sturdy staff with gold bands at both ends. "What's this?" She gripped it and tried to pull it nearer, then yelped with surprise at its weight. Her hand fit easily around it, but it seemed to weigh as much as a building.

"*Ru Yi Jing Gu Bang*. The magic staff of Sun Wukong. Weighs seven tons, and it inspired magic staff-makers to give most of them this functionality." Taylor looked down at the blue fire staff and tightened his hands. It shrunk to the size of a pin, and he tucked it behind his ear. "Okay, we'd better quit playing around and pick out some weapons. What were you thinking?"

Julie glanced at the sword Taylor had picked up earlier.

Yeah, that looks like a good idea, Hat told her.

She bent down and gripped the white hilt. "What about—"

"Julie, wait!"

Taylor's yelp came a moment too late. Julie had pulled the blade from the scabbard. It was a short, compact sword with a leaf-shaped blade, of which Julie caught only a glimpse before the steel caught fire. With a muted roar, gold flames licked the blade, casting wild shadows across the Warehouse. The flames rushed toward the white hilt, and Julie let out a yelp and let it go. It fell to the floor with a clatter, once again polished steel.

"What..." She turned to Taylor, gaping.

"I tried to warn you." Taylor was peering at her. "It caught fire!"

"No shit!" Julie poked the sword with one toe. "Why? Also, Hat, what was that about?"

Hat snickered.

"That's the interesting part." Taylor rubbed the back of his neck. "That was Dyrnwyn."

"Dyrnwyn!" Julie crouched to study the sword. "The Sword of Rhydderch Hael?"

"How do you *know* this stuff?" Taylor groaned.

"I read a lot. Dude, this sword is only supposed to burst into flame if someone who is worthy or well-born holds it." Julie smirked. "Guess that means I'm worthy since I'm definitely not well-born."

Taylor sighed. "I'm not going to hear the end of this, am I?"

"Nope." Julie straightened. "Besides, I know better than to take a sword into a fight. You keep saying my footwork isn't ready yet."

Taylor chuckled. "It isn't. Don't look at me like that."

"Fine. Why don't *you* take Dyrnwyn, and I'll find something else?" Julie retorted.

"To your left," Hat suggested. "I think the weapons over there are more your speed."

Julie looked to her left and spotted a row of sturdy black plastic crates on a shelf a few yards away. "Okay, but if anything catches fire, I'm throwing you into it," she told Hat as she went over to them.

"Dyrnwyn?" Taylor glanced at it. "I don't think so, but this'll do." He fished a blade with a deep-green scabbard out of the heap.

"What's that, Excalibur?" Julie opened the first crate and grinned at the object inside.

"Don't make me laugh." Hat snorted. "That weedy elf wouldn't be able to pick up Excalibur, let alone draw it from a stone."

"Or a magic hat pretending to be a stone." Julie looked over her shoulder at Taylor. "I think I found my weapon."

"Need I remind you that I'm far more than a magic hat?" Hat growled.

"What is it?" Taylor asked, belting the scabbard around his waist.

"It's a big-ass gun, is what it is." Julie lifted it out of the crate and adjusted the weight in her palm. She pointed the muzzle at the floor and kept her trigger finger on the barrel.

"Looks like it's not the first time you've handled one of those." Taylor came closer. "I think it's going to come in handy."

"It's not. Dad used to take me shooting." Julie shook the memory off before it could bring her to tears. "What is it, anyway? Nine-mil?"

"Oh, no. It's magic. It shoots the proper ammunition to affect the paranormal you're fighting," Taylor explained.

"So, silver for werewolves and garlic for vampires?"

"Pretty much." Taylor grimaced. "Please try not to shoot any vampires. We're supposed to be rescuing one, remember?"

"Top shelf," Hat told Julie. "There's something up there you'll need."

Julie reached up and retrieved a handful of silver spheres about the size of a walnut. "What do they do?"

"They reopen portals that have recently been closed," Hat explained. "Since you've been thinking that Malcolm was taken through a portal, given the way his scent disappeared."

"Excuse me, but I've had enough of mind-reading for one day." Julie slipped the spheres into her pocket.

"Take those handcuffs over there, too," Hat added. "They're magical restraints. They switch off a person's magic."

"Cool." Julie grabbed the cuffs, which glowed a faint blue.

Taylor appeared at her side, holding out a belt with a holster. "I think your gun will fit in here."

"Thanks." Julie secured the belt around her hips. "What magical stuff does your sword do?"

Taylor laughed as they headed for the doors. "It's very sharp, and it cuts stuff."

"Sounds good to me." Julie smirked. "There's one more thing we need."

"What's that?" Taylor paused at the door.

Julie grinned. "A unit of werewolf soldiers."

Six wolves jumped out of Julie's Mustang and Taylor's Mitsubishi with their tails wagging and their claws clicking on the paving as they bounded into the courtyard of the Nox mansion. They circled the cars, yipping and snapping at each other. It looked incongruous among the rosebushes that lined the courtyard and the spruce trees that rose beyond the looming white walls surrounding it.

Slamming the door of Genevieve, the 1971 Mustang Mach-1 she rented from her landlady, Julie looked past the walls at the mansion that towered above the trees beyond. Its one-way glass windows shimmered in the sunlight. The last time she'd been here, Malcolm Nox had been safely in his suite, playing a video game.

Are you sure about this? Hat muttered.

Julie turned her attention back to the werewolves. Two of them were tussling, rolling over each other and biting at paws and furry necks. Only Isaiah seemed to be doing anything. He had his nose down to the ground, golden tail curled over his back and waving slightly.

Give them a minute, she told Hat. *They're a little excited.*

A little? Hat grumbled. *I still can't believe Kaplan let you take them.*

Think of it as a field trip. Good for their training, Julie pointed out.

Training? They've had two days of boot camp! They should be in the gym punching bags, not out here trying to find the heir to the vampire throne! Hat spluttered.

Look, Hat, we needed backup, and, like Kaplan said, he's short on agents he can trust right now. The Weres are innocent since they were in Montana when the Yetis broke into HQ. Julie shrugged. *They're better than nothing, and we need their noses.*

Taylor stepped out of the satellite-silver Mitsubishi Evolution IV he was driving today. Julie thought he changed his cars more often than his underwear. "Okay, Julie. What's the plan?"

Isaiah raised his shaggy head and pricked his triangle ears toward Julie. He gave a brief howl, and the other Weres quit fooling around and looked at her.

"I'm going to start by talking to the staff." Julie gestured at Taylor. "Taylor's going to get online with Malcolm's gamer buddies. If anyone knows where he's gone, they will." She waved at the wolves. "You guys need to cast around for his scent. I know Julius tried, but werewolves have the best sense of smell in the paranormal world."

Isaiah wagged his tail and nodded. He let out a series of barks, and the werewolves split up into teams of two. Two of the teams trotted through the courtyard gate. Austin and Chester stayed behind and began to search a grid, noses to the ground.

"Okay, maybe the Weres weren't the worst idea," Taylor conceded as he and Julie walked toward the mansion.

A long-faced butler wearing a morning suit, a muffler pulled up over his nose, and a broad black hat to shield his vampire skin from the sun, was holding the courtyard gate for them. Julie paused and put a hand on his shoulder. "Gerald, I'm really sorry about Malcolm. We're going to do our best to find him."

The butler nodded miserably. "I know you care about him, too, miss. Please do whatever you can. Master Julius is with Captain Kaplan, trying to track down whoever did this. I'm most worried about Master Malcolm."

"We'll find him," Julie promised.

"With the handfasting so soon..." Gerald seemed close to tears. "Please, miss!"

Julie gritted her teeth and strode past him and through the fragrant rose garden toward the mansion. Malcolm Nox might have gotten himself into this, but she was going to get him out of it.

Taylor tugged at Hat's brim. *Could you stop that?*

Stop what? Hat shot back.

You're wriggling. It's really annoying. Taylor followed the butler down a long, grandiose hallway.

Sorry if I'm an ancient magical artifact and not an ordinary hat, Hat retorted.

Taylor stifled a sigh. *I wish Julie had done this part.*

You're better at video games than talking to people, Hat jeered.

Gerald stopped outside a door and pushed it open. "Master Malcolm's suite, sir. I'm afraid I don't know any of his passwords. I'm not sure how you're going to connect with his online acquaintances."

"Thanks, Gerald." Taylor tried for a reassuring smile. "It's okay. I have ways and means." He tapped Hat, who was a ridiculous top hat with a bright purple ribbon that clashed with the green shirt and black jeans Taylor had changed into before they left HQ.

Gerald glanced at Hat but elected not to comment. "Thank you, sir."

Taylor stepped into Malcolm's suite. It was nicer than

Taylor's, with a huge couch facing a massive screen on one wall. To Taylor's shame, it was less messy than his rooms at home.

"Hey, Gerald—" he began, but when he turned around, the butler had disappeared like smoke.

"Creep," Hat commented.

"You're one to talk." Taylor tugged Hat off and tossed him on the back of the couch, then sat down and picked up a controller. The game booted up, but as Taylor had feared, its online function was password-protected.

"Leave this to me." Hat let out soft beeps and hums like an old modem. "There!"

The game unlocked, and Malcolm's avatar appeared on the screen, a burly ginger guy in camouflage clutching a heavy weapon and breathing heavily in that weird video-game-character way. Taylor pulled on the headphones and turned left and right, saying nothing. A few moments later, an unfamiliar voice spoke.

"Ed, my dude! Where have you been?"

Another avatar had run up to Taylor's on the screen, a tall black guy with tattoos. Two others joined him. Taylor was willing to bet ItzMeZee189, JK1997, and GothChick50 didn't look anything like their avatars in real life.

"Dude, you left us in the shit back there!" JK snapped, his gamer tag lighting up to indicate that he was the one speaking. "What were you thinking?"

"Shut up. He's dealing with some shit. You know that," Goth-Chick snapped.

"You okay, bro?" ItzMeZee asked.

"I'm afraid not." Taylor took a deep breath. They were probably humans. "Your friend has gone missing. I'm from the FBI," he added, picking an agency at random. "I'm trying to figure out where he's gone and what's happened to him."

"Ed? *Missing?*" GothChick squawked.

Taylor glanced at the tag above Malcolm's avatar and couldn't help smirking. DefinitelyNotEdward1897? Seriously?

"I need to know if any of you noticed strange behavior from Mal...from Ed in the last few days," Taylor told them.

"I mean, Ed's kind of moody," ItzMeZee conceded.

JK sighed. "But the way he acted last night was just weird."

"Last night? What did he do?" Taylor asked.

"He randomly logged off when we were deep into a side quest. Left us all in trouble. I died and lost a bunch of stuff!" JK grumbled.

"He was weird about it, too," GothChick added. "He just said, 'I've got to go,' and he was gone. No joking around, nothing. Just left."

"Did he mention anything specific that was bothering him? Or anywhere he was planning to go?" Taylor prodded.

ItzMeZee sighed. "Dude, Ed and I have been playing together for, like, five years, and I don't even know his real name. He's super private about his personal life. I don't think he'd have told us even if he did have a plan."

Taylor chewed the inside of his cheek. "What time did he disappear?"

"It was early for Ed. One in the morning. He loves all-nighters," ItzMeZee supplied.

"You'll let us know, right?" GothChick added. "When you find him?"

"He'll let you know himself when he logs back into the game," Taylor assured her. "Thanks for your help."

He pulled off the headphones as Julie walked in. The corner of her lip twitched at the sight of the top hat on the back of the couch. "Seriously, Hat? You had to embarrass Taylor?"

Hat sniffed. "I'm not sorry."

Julie picked him up. With a soft *poof*, he transformed back into the stylish fedora she'd been wearing earlier, and she replaced him on her head. "Any luck, Taylor?"

"None." Taylor put down the headphones and the controller. "I think his buddies are humans. He didn't tell them anything. All I could find out was that he disappeared around one in the morning."

"That was a few minutes after Gerald brought him dinner." Julie bit her lip the way she did when she was thinking, her bright eyes distant. "The staff didn't see anything, either. Gerald's distraught."

The sounds of scrabbling paws and panting came from the hallway, and the six werewolves burst into the suite, filled with mad energy. Teddy, stout and red-furred in his wolf form, sniffed a pile of clothes on the floor. Austin found a dirty plate and licked it.

"Austin, gross!" Julie protested.

Isaiah trotted into the room and transformed into human form halfway to Julie.

Julie sent up silent thanks for whatever magic their uniforms contained that saved her from seeing freshly shifted butt as he got his breath back and smoothed his blue uniform. "Did you find anything?"

He shook his head. "No, ma'am. We didn't find much more than Mr. Nox did. Malcolm went over a wall where there was a gap in the mansion's security. He got a couple blocks into the human part of the suburbs, then his scent disappeared."

"Doesn't disappear." Teddy had returned to his human form, too. "It gets lost in a cloud of portal smell."

Isaiah wrinkled his nose. "That stuff reeks. He was definitely taken through a portal. You were right."

Julie narrowed her eyes. Taylor stifled a groan. That was never a good sign.

CHAPTER FIVE

The Weres spilled into the courtyard ahead of Julie and Taylor, barking and bumping into one another. Julie's mind raced. It was clear what had happened, but their mission wasn't to investigate. It was to bring Malcolm Nox home.

"There's only one next step." Julie reached into her pocket and pulled out one of the portal-reopening spheres. "We've got to go through that portal and see where Malcolm went."

Taylor folded his arms. He was leaning against Genevieve's hood. The Mustang's pewter paint shimmered in the sunlight. "Let's think about this for a second, Julie. I agree we need to reopen the portal, but should we go through it? It could lead anywhere."

"Julius and Kaplan want us to find Malcolm." Julie closed her hand over the sphere, enjoying its cool, round pressure in her palm. "Anyway, we've got backup."

It was a pity that Chester chose that moment to flop down on the ground and scratch his ear with a hind paw while Noah cocked a leg against the wheel of Taylor's car.

"Yeah." Taylor grunted. "Backup."

"You got any better ideas?" Julie fished out her car keys. "Get your fat ass off Genevieve and let's go."

Squealing tires cut Taylor's protests short. Julie looked up. The mansion's gate opened, and with a screech of rubber, a cherry-red Porsche Carrera spun into the courtyard.

Julie tensed. "*Cassidy.*"

Taylor gripped her arm to stop her from reaching for the gun at her hip. "Take it easy," he murmured.

"Do I need to remind you that the last time I saw Malcolm's fiancée, she tried to rip my throat out and not figuratively?" Julie snapped. "This time, Malcolm's not here to stop her."

"She's Quickening too, remember? We need to keep her calm." Taylor's hand was on the hilt of his sword.

Isaiah let out a low growl as the Porsche jerked to a halt on the other side of the courtyard. The six wolves surrounded Julie and Taylor, their hackles up, and crouched as if to leap.

The Porsche's door banged open, and Taylor let go of Julie's arm. The recruiter gripped the gun tightly.

"She's Quickening," Hat repeated. "She's not going to be reasonable."

"I have some sympathy for her, but I don't have time for her bullshit," Julie shot back.

The gorgeous young vampire flung herself out of the Porsche, her black hair swinging like a cape around her slender torso. Underneath the brim of her wide hat and through the thin veil over her face, Cassidy's red eyes burned brightly when they landed on Julie.

"*YOU!*" she shouted, striding across the courtyard in knee-length boots and pointing a white-gloved hand.

Julie saw a claw rip through the tip of the glove as Cassidy's vampire powers overwhelmed her. She ripped the gun out of the holster and held it out, not aiming it, but feeling a crackle of magic through the metal in her hands as it calibrated for a vampire.

Metal sang as it touched metal. Taylor had drawn his sword, and the polished blade caught the sunlight.

"Stop right there, Cassidy!" Julie yelled. She aimed at Cassidy's chest when the vampire continued to hurtle toward them. "You're three steps away from getting ashed!"

Hat trembled on her head. The crouching wolves let out a chorus of snarls, and Cassidy stumbled to a halt. Her piercing scarlet eyes didn't leave Julie's face.

"You took him." Cassidy's voice was low and animal, a throaty growl. It made Julie think of the human blood that must have passed through that throat, donated or not. "*You took Malcolm!*"

"Calm down," Julie snapped.

She's Quickening. She can't! Hat hissed.

So everyone keeps telling me, but we're all better than our biology, Julie shot back. She kept her voice steady. "I didn't take Malcolm, Cassidy. I'm trying to find him."

"So, you *do* want him." Cassidy spat the words, fangs flashing.

"Want him?" Julie barked a laugh. "As if. I care about Malcolm, and I think he could be more than he imagines someday, but I am *not* interested in him."

Cassidy hissed, the sound part snake, part cat. She took a stalking step nearer, and Isaiah's growl rose in pitch and volume.

"Come on, Cassidy. I'm not chasing down your man. I'm not interested in him, and I never have been." Julie cocked the gun with a satisfying metallic click. "I told you not to take another step."

Cassidy stopped, but her eyes did not leave Julie's throat. She wondered if the vampire could sense the blood pulsing through her carotid.

"Malcolm's not interested in me either," Julie added. "You're the one he's marrying, Cassidy. Think about it. At the factory the other night, Malcolm didn't want to put you in danger. He was protecting you. He loves *you.*"

Silence hung over the courtyard, underlined by the wolves' soft growls.

Taylor's voice rang across the courtyard. "You've got two options. You can either believe that and help us find Malcolm before he gets killed by the Yetis he's been hunting—and trust me, those Yetis are more than capable of doing that—or you can leave and let us get on with our job."

Cassidy's fingers flexed inside her gloves, and she ran her tongue over her lips, fangs showing again. Julie swallowed hard and applied half a pound of pressure to the trigger. *I don't want to have to explain to Malcolm how I had to kill his fiancée.*

The vampire's eyes did not waver. She took a step closer. Julie applied more pressure to the trigger, ready to pull. Taylor slipped into a fighting crouch, sword raised in plow guard. Isaiah's lips pulled back from his long white teeth, growl intensifying.

Cassidy raised her hands, buried her face in them, and burst into tears.

The wolves' growls switched off. Julie and Taylor exchanged glances.

Uh, wasn't expecting that, Hat mumbled.

Julie lowered her gun but kept it by her side. "Cassidy?"

The vampire didn't respond. She leaned against Genevieve and cried harder. Great racking sobs shook her skinny frame from her high-heeled boots to the top of her glossy head.

"Cassidy?" Julie holstered her gun and took a step forward.

Taylor touched her shoulder. "Julie, no. It could be a trick."

Julie shook him off. "I don't think so."

Julie— Hat began.

You and I have had this conversation, Hat, she shot back. She stepped around Isaiah, whose hackles were lowering, and cautiously approached Cassidy. The vampire continued to weep.

"Hey." Julie touched Cassidy's shoulder. "It's going to be okay. We're going to find him."

Cassidy sobbed harder.

"C'mon, Cassidy." Julie tentatively put her arm around the bony shoulders. "Take deep breaths. We'll find Malcolm. For all we know, he's defeating those Yetis as we speak. It's going to be okay."

Cassidy lowered her hands, raising a tear-streaked face. The scarlet of her eyes had dimmed, replaced by ordinary redness around the lids. Tears cascaded down her cheeks. "Oh, Malcolm!" she cried out.

"This isn't helping him." Julie gave her a soft squeeze. "Dry your eyes, Cassidy. We've got to go find him. We're going to do everything we can, okay? We'll bring him home to you in one piece."

Taylor and the werewolves gaped at her. Taylor sheathed his sword.

Cassidy's words were interrupted by her sobs. "Why are you…being so…nice to me? I've been a total…bitch to you since I…met you."

Julie lowered her arm and stepped in front of the vampire to meet her eyes. "Are you going to continue being bitchy?"

Cassidy looked at her, reaching inside her veil with a gloved hand to wipe away her tears. "No."

Julie shrugged. "Then I see no reason why we shouldn't make a fresh start." She put her hands on her hips. "When did you last speak to Malcolm?"

Cassidy's face screwed up again, and she sobbed harder. Chester, who was the size of a pony in wolf form, trotted up to her and thrust his wet nose against her hand. Cassidy took a deep breath and stuttered out the words. "Last night…early…but that's not…that's not unusual." She sucked in another breath. "I can't feel him, Julie. *I can't feel him.*"

Julie stifled a groan. This wasn't the time for romantic nonsense. "What did he say when you spoke to him?"

"No. You don't understand." Cassidy shook her head, then

shoved her hand under her veil again to wipe her nose. "I always know where Malcolm is. *Exactly* where he is."

Julie scanned her orb training. It didn't mention that in the vampire senses section. "Uh..."

"We did a pre-handfasting ritual. Traditional among vampires, and, well, I really wanted it." Cassidy managed another breath. "We exchanged blood. As a result, I can sense Malcolm's presence. I'm connected to him."

"Okay. That makes sense." Julie nodded.

"Only, for the past few hours, I haven't been able to sense him." Tears rose in Cassidy's eyes, threatening to spill over again. "I went back to the last place I could sense him, in Central Park." She gestured. "B-but I couldn't feel him. It's like he's on the other side of the world." Her voice cracked. "Or he's not in the world."

Julie bit her lip hard at those words. No. She couldn't allow herself to think they were too late. "Does distance affect the connection?"

"Yes, but I can feel him wherever he is in the city. I've never lost my connection to him before." Cassidy's voice was brimming with tears. "I came here to ask Julius for help. It's driving me a little crazy."

A little? Hat snorted.

"Our handfasting is tomorrow." Cassidy sagged against Genevieve, hiding her face in her hands again. "I've loved him since I first laid eyes on him in the second grade at private school. Oh, Julie, what am I going to do if we can't get him back? I-I never thought he...he would ask me to...to marry him." Sobs racked her body again. "What am I supposed to do if the person I've loved since...since I was a little girl is taken...away from me *forever?*"

Wheels turned in Julie's mind. *She really does love him,* she told Hat. *This is more than the Quickening.*

Hat scoffed. *Turns out Vampzilla has a heart after all.*

Really? You're going to be snarky now? Julie bit her lip. *We've got to get moving and get him back. I'm freaked out that he's not in the city anymore.*

She left Cassidy petting Chester and turned to Taylor, gesturing for him to join her. Isaiah blossomed into his human form and followed them to a corner by Cassidy's Porsche.

"I have a plan," Julie announced.

"This is going to be good," Taylor muttered in resignation.

She shot him a look, but Isaiah folded his arms and nodded firmly. "What is it?"

"Cassidy's connection thing seems legit. If she can't sense Malcolm, he's gone through a portal." She squared her shoulders. "I think he's gone through multiple portals."

"Yeah, he must have," Isaiah interjected. "We lost his scent two blocks from here. If he'd gotten into a car, we would have known. I think he took a portal to Central Park and another portal elsewhere."

Julie nodded. "We have to go to wherever she last sensed him, reopen *that* portal, and go in there and get him. Cassidy will be able to lead us to him. If he's being held by Yetis, we'll have to bust in and fight our way to him."

"Julie, that portal could lead anywhere," Taylor cautioned in a low voice. "Anywhere in Avalon or the human world."

Julie looked up at him. "Are you with me, Taylor?"

He didn't break eye contact, just sighed. "Of course I am. I mean, when have I missed out on a crazy-ass Julie plan?"

Julie smirked. "Fabulous. Let's go."

Genevieve had three hundred and seventy-five horses in her 429 V8 Cobrajet engine, and they were all chomping at the bit.

The Mustang roared with anticipation at the red light. Julie drummed her fingers on the wheel, casting hungry glances toward Central Park. The drive from the Nox mansion in Staten Island had never felt longer.

"She's a beaut," Isaiah murmured from the passenger seat. He ran his fingers over the dashboard. "What's her top speed?"

"I'm doing my best not to find out." Julie grinned. "I'm just borrowing her from my landlady."

Chester thrust his head between Julie and Isaiah. "I vote you race Taylor to the next light."

Teddy joined him. "Never mind him. Race Cassidy. That Porsche goes from zero to sixty in four seconds flat."

Julie glanced sideways at Taylor, who was sharing the Mitsubishi with Noah and Blake. The car gleamed with care, but Genevieve could smoke him if she wanted to. For a moment, she considered it, then decided today was not the day. "Sorry, guys. Sometime when we're not on a life-or-death mission."

"Fine." Teddy sighed.

"And put on your seat belts. I don't want any fines today, okay?" Julie added.

Grumbling, the two younger Weres strapped in. Julie relented as the light turned green. She put her foot down, and Genevieve let out a deafening roar, surging forward. Excited whooping and howling filled the car, and Taylor was left in the dust.

CHAPTER SIX

"I'd have thought they would take Malcolm to the Avalon portal," Julie commented.

The Maine Monument towered over them as they followed one of the park's concrete paths among the green lawns. The gold Columbia at the top of the monument shimmered in the sunshine.

They couldn't just walk into Avalon Village with a kidnapped prince, could they? Hat reasoned.

Makes sense. Julie shrugged. "Okay, Cassidy. Where was it?"

"Somewhere around here." Cassidy turned left and right, straightening her veil to avoid the bright summer sunshine. "I can't pinpoint where."

"We can." Isaiah stepped forward, glancing around for people. He gestured at the other Weres. "Fan out. Human form. Our senses are duller then, but we'll find him. The air reeks of him here."

The other werewolves scattered, and Julie turned to Taylor. "How are we going to avoid these humans seeing us open a magic portal?" She gestured at the knot of tourists gaping at the monument.

"I can do a spell for that." Taylor reached behind his ear and held up the pin-sized magic staff. "It's basic for Aether Elves. Even a lazy ass like me picks that up in magic class."

"A concealing spell?" Julie guessed.

Taylor nodded. "An illusion, basically. Not a strong one, but it'll hold long enough. We just need to hustle once we open the portal."

"Thanks." Julie hesitated. "Hey, and thanks for being part of my crazy-ass plans."

Taylor shrugged, raising both hands. "Crazy-ass plans are the spice of life, right?"

Julie laughed.

Are you going to check in with Kaplan? Hat asked. *I think he'd appreciate it, and it'll make this marginally safer.*

"Yeah, good idea." Julie tugged out her phone and dialed the captain's number.

"Kaplan," he growled in her ear.

"Hey, Captain. It's me," Julie chirped.

"I'm aware, Meadows. I am capable of reading a caller ID. What do you want?" Kaplan grumbled.

Julie stifled her grin. "We've tracked Malcolm to Central Park South near the Maine Monument. We're going to reopen the portal and follow him through. I've got Cassidy with me, too."

Kaplan muttered something too softly for Julie to hear, but it sounded like, "That psycho bitch?" Louder, he said, "Okay, Meadows. Keep me updated. I can't be there. I'm tracking down a handful of scientists and IT trolls who have been conspicuously absent from work today. IA hasn't made any progress on finding the traitor."

"Good luck, sir." Julie meant it.

"You too. Be careful, Meadows," Kaplan added gruffly.

Julie smirked. "Aw, thanks, Captain. I'm beginning to think you care."

"I just don't want to lose my best recruiters or spend time and money mopping up what's left of you," Kaplan growled. "Goodbye."

"Bye." Julie hung up.

"Here!" Teddy was crouching on one of the lawns and he straightened, gesturing. "The trail disappears here."

Julie put a hand on her gun. Taylor's sword shimmered with the strength of the illusion that had been cast on it during forging, as he'd explained earlier. They followed Cassidy and the werewolves to where Teddy was waiting. Isaiah sniffed the air. "I agree. This is it."

"This feels right." Cassidy's words came out as a hiss. When Julie looked at her, her eyes had turned scarlet again, and the vampire's fangs were growing.

"Get it together, Cassidy," Julie growled.

Taylor had fished the magic staff out from behind his ear again.

I don't think she can *get it together*, Hat grumbled.

"Malcolllmm," Cassidy hissed. "I neeed to find Malcolllmm!"

"Ready?" Taylor held up the tiny staff.

Julie pulled out one of the spheres. *Hat, how do I do this?*

You didn't think it wise to ask earlier? Hat snarked.

Cassidy was beginning to drool. She sucked on her fangs, flexing her hands inside her gloves.

Hat! Julie glanced at the tourists.

Okay, okay! Just shake it in your hand like a die and toss it, Hat explained. *It'll reopen the portal when it hits the right spot.*

Okay. Julie nodded at Taylor. He shot a look at the tourists, who were still engrossed in the monument, and made a flicking motion with the tiny staff, muttering in a language Julie didn't recognize. The air between them and the tourists shimmered like a heat haze.

Cassidy grabbed Julie's arm. She could feel the woman's claws digging into her skin. "*Malcolllmm,*" the vampire hissed.

"Cool it!" Julie shook the sphere in her hand and threw it, and the air rippled, making a faint sizzling noise. She stepped forward, reached out, and felt the faint tingle as it disappeared into the portal. Beyond, her fingers felt cold air.

"Yes!" Cassidy lunged forward.

Julie grabbed her arm. "Easy!"

"I'll go first." Isaiah squared his shoulders and stepped forward. After slipping into their wolf forms, the rest of the pack followed.

Julie glanced at Taylor, who grinned. "I'm right behind you."

"Okay." She kept a grip on Cassidy's arm. "Let's go and find Malcolm."

She strode forward with a confidence she didn't feel, and the familiar tingle of portal magic spread across her skin, along with a disorienting sensation of the ground sinking under her feet. Blinking against her blurred vision, Julie stepped into an underground cavern. The Weres, to her intense relief, were just ahead of her, sniffing the ground. She noticed patches of ice here and there. The air was bitterly cold, and dim light seeped into the cavern. She could see faint cracks far above and a layer of what seemed to be blue ice.

She let out a breath she hadn't realized she'd been holding. A cloud of steam surrounded her face.

"Malcolm." Cassidy turned to her, red eyes wide. "He was here."

"He was," Isaiah confirmed, looking up. The hackles on his strong shoulders had half-risen. "Not long ago, either."

"He's not far away." Cassidy's breath hitched, and her eyes glowed. "He's hurt. I must find himm!"

"We know." Julie laid a hand on her gun. "Which way?"

Cassidy pointed directly ahead of them, where narrower caves branched off like tunnels. "That one."

Julie nodded. "Let's go."

"Noah, Teddy, flank the bipeds," Isaiah barked. "Austin, Blake, you take the rear. Chester, with me."

Taylor kept a hand on the hilt of his sword as they moved across the cavern. Something quietly creaked above them. When Julie glanced up, she wondered if she could see cracks in the ice. Stalagmites and stalactites jutted from the floor and ceiling of the cavern. Tiny drops of water fell on them, their eerie *plinks* echoing through the vast space. Apart from that, the cavern was silent, and their footsteps sounded deafening.

"You said Malcolm is hurt," Julie murmured to Cassidy. "Can you sense how badly?"

Cassidy turned glowing eyes to her. "No. But I will find himm." Her jutting fangs were impeding her speech. "And I will rip the throat out of whoever hurt himm."

They reached the mouth of the narrower cave and Cassidy shoved forward, pushing Isaiah and Chester aside. "Malllcolmm!" she shrieked.

"Shhhh!" Julie hissed.

Isaiah's jaws snapped shut on Cassidy's boot to stop her from rushing down the dark tunnel ahead of them. Julie seized her by the back of her leather jacket and hauled her back. "Cassidy. *Cassidy! Calm down!*"

"Unhand me, human!" Cassidy spat, swiping at Julie with both hands. Fingernails extended into catlike claws that hissed through the air with a deadly edge.

"Cut that out!" Taylor grabbed Cassidy's wrists. "If you want to find Malcolm, you've got to stay with us. Understand?"

Cassidy bared her fangs, revealing row upon row of teeth ending in needle tips.

"Listen to him, Cassidy," Julie growled. "What are you going to do if Malcolm is being held captive by all those Yetis? Fight them on your own? You need us. Stay with us."

Cassidy relented. Her teeth shrank, and when she blinked, the redness in her eyes dissipated a little. "Okay," she mumbled.

Taylor let go of her wrists but kept a wary eye on her.

"Let's go," Julie told the werewolves.

Isaiah gave Cassidy a last glance before stepping forward, nose just above the ground, ears twitching. They advanced down the dark tunnel. It was even quieter here, and the floor was rough under their feet. The tunnel twisted this way and that. Julie kept a hand on the rocky wall to navigate. Cassidy's heavy breathing filled the air. Julie could just make out the shaggy silhouettes of the two werewolves leading the way.

"Faster," Cassidy hissed. "He's weakening."

"Let's pick up the pace, guys," Julie called.

Nails clicking on the rock, Isaiah and Chester broke into a trot. Julie jogged after them, the gun bumping her hip. Taylor's sword jingled in its scabbard beside her. Julie heard something skittering in the distance.

"What was that?" she hissed.

"I don't know," Austin admitted. "I've never smelled anything like it."

"Smells...rabbity," Blake offered.

Hat? Julie asked.

Before Hat could answer, Isaiah snarled. "Yetis up ahead. Still some distance away, but I can smell them."

"It's not like we weren't expect—ah!" Julie's foot caught on a rock, and she stumbled forward. Taylor grabbed her arm and hauled her to her feet before she fell. The convoy stumbled to a halt.

"Are you okay?" Taylor asked anxiously.

Julie shook off his arm. "I'm fine. Just a rock."

"Sorry. I should have warned you." Chester looked back, ears flattening sheepishly. "I forgot you couldn't see. The terrain is getting rougher."

Taylor fished the staff out from behind his ear.

"I'm not sure that's a good idea." Julie glanced around. "Blue fire might catch some attention."

"I'm not thinking of fire." Taylor touched the staff, and it blossomed to its full height. The gemstone glowed dully. He frowned in concentration. Soundlessly, the shadows in the tunnel drew back like the Red Sea, opening a path of soft light on the ground ahead of Julie.

About time, Hat grumbled.

"That's pretty cool. How'd you do that?" Julie asked.

Taylor shrugged. "I *am* an Elf of the Mystical Dusk."

"Who didn't pay attention in magic class," Julie reminded him.

Taylor sighed. "An elf needs to have *some* secrets."

Cassidy was fidgeting. She ripped off her veil and gloves. "Let's go!"

"Yeah, let's." Julie touched Cassidy's arm. "Stay with us, okay?"

"I can go much faster than you," Cassidy growled. "I can get to him quickly."

"Yeah, well, cool it," Julie warned. "You need us, remember?"

They jogged onward, Julie's feet sure on the rocks now that she could see where she was going. She moved in her own little bubble of light, thanks to Taylor's magic.

It's embarrassing to be the only one who can't see in the dark. Julie ducked beneath a rock jutting from the roof of the cavern and skirted a shimmering patch of blue ice.

I don't think humans have ever been here. We're deep in Avalon, Hat told her.

Julie shivered. Despite the effort they were expending, the cold was seeping through her clothes. Hat stirred on her head, and soft woolen folds wrapped around her ears. Supernatural heat radiated from him, instantly warming her.

Thanks, Hat. Julie smiled.

Someone's got to take care of the pathetic human, Hat muttered.

Ahead, the Weres jumped over a pile of rocks in the middle of the tunnel. Julie scrambled over it after them and found that the tunnel curved sharply to the right. The Weres had slowed down and were sniffing around.

"Outta my way!" Cassidy snapped, her words slurring around her fangs. She shoved past Julie, pushing forward. "He's close!"

"Miss, don't!" Isaiah snapped.

Cassidy shoved past him, and something hurtled toward her from the shadows with a whistling shriek. Isaiah roared as he charged forward, but Cassidy had already seized the *thing* in both hands and was holding it up. It shrieked, spitting and clawing at her face, its lithe, furry body whipping from side to side. Julie had her gun in her hands and felt the magical crackle as it calibrated, but she hesitated. What if she missed?

Chester leaped, his form ghostly in the faint light. His jaws snapped shut on the creature's lower body, and with one shake and a final pig-like shriek, it was over.

Julie gasped. "What *was* that?"

Cassidy looked at the blood smeared on the ground, and her claws grew longer. "Malcolm!" she snarled.

Taylor grabbed her arm before she could dash forward. "Yes, Malcolm! Stay with me, Cassidy. Come on. We've got to work together!"

Julie kept her gun in her hands as she tiptoed to the dead creature. In Taylor's pale light, it had a long, thin, supple body covered in greenish fur and small rat-like claws. It might have been an elongated weasel if not for the snub piggy nose.

"It's a ramidreju," Hat supplied. "They probably dug through most of this cave over the past few centuries, looking for gold."

An ancient creature obsessed with gold, Julie's orb training told her. *Early humans believed their fur had healing properties.*

"I guess it's attacking us because of its gold being somewhere nearby?" Julie prodded it with a toe.

"It?" Hat gave a dark chuckle. "Try 'they.'"

Isaiah's growl echoed from just ahead. Julie jogged around the bend in the tunnel, and the others stayed close behind.

"Shit!" Taylor let go of Cassidy's arm.

"That about sums it up." Julie raised her gun.

Isaiah was standing in the middle of the tunnel, hackles raised. It widened into a cave around them, and the walls were pocked with small, dark holes. From the holes, a hundred pairs of yellow eyes watched them from behind piggy snouts.

"Isn't there another way to Malcolm?" Julie hissed, cocking her gun.

Cassidy turned wild eyes to her. "He's in pain. There's no time."

"I guess we take this route, then," Julie replied.

Taylor held up the staff and a blue flame appeared over the gem, flickering silently and illuminating the cavern. There were hisses and yips from the ramidreju, which drew back into their holes. Julie eyed the other end of the cave. It was another tunnel, this time devoid of holes.

"And of gold," Hat added, reading her mind. "If you can get to that tunnel, they'll leave you alone."

Julie glanced at Taylor. "Are we making a run for it?"

Cassidy stepped forward, hissing.

Taylor sighed. "I don't think we have much choice."

"Okay." Julie took a deep breath. "Go!"

Isaiah leaped forward with a howl that echoed around the cavern. Immediately, the floors and walls swarmed with ramidreju, their claws clattering, their yips and oinks filling the air. Julie let out a desperate yell and fired beyond Isaiah and Chester in a series of deafening cracks. In the flickering blue light, the ramidreju scattered, but more swarmed around her feet, snapping at her boots.

"Die, sucker!" she yelled, stomping on one. Its squeal was cut short.

Taylor swung his staff like a club, sending three of them flying as they bolted across the cavern. Cassidy plucked one out of the air and threw it aside, almost hitting Julie. A furry body twined around her ankles and she tumbled to the ground, rolled, and came up firing as a shrieking ramidreju launched at her face. The bullet tore through its body, vaporizing it in a disturbing cloud of gold dust.

"Gross, gross, gross!" Julie squealed, rolling to her feet. Gold dust covered her like glitter.

"Almost there!" Taylor yelled, swiping at another one with his staff. Isaiah had one on his back. He snapped at it as he ran but didn't slow down. Chester flung himself sideways to slam his shoulder into the creature, and it tumbled off Isaiah's back and fell under their claws. They tore it to shreds, and Cassidy pushed past them and rushed into the tunnel.

"Cassidy, wait!" Julie yelled. She grabbed the vampire by the jacket and spun her against the wall. The Weres came with them and tumbled into the tunnel. Taylor dispatched the last of the ramidreju with a brief swing of his staff. The others stopped at the mouth of the tunnel, still grunting and squealing, then disappeared back into their holes.

There was a breathless silence, then Taylor's blue fire filled the cavern.

"That was disturbing," Julie managed. "Isaiah, are you okay?"

The golden wolf's fur was streaked with blood, but he nodded. "Let's keep going."

Taylor held up the flaming staff. Ahead, the tunnel grew narrower.

Great. Julie sighed inwardly. *A dungeon crawl while I'm babysitting a mad vamp. Exactly what we need.*

At least this should slow Cassidy down a little, Hat suggested.

Isaiah trotted forward, lowering his head and crouching to fit through the gap. Julie holstered her gun and followed at a crouch as long as she could, then dropped to her hands and knees. The rocks scraped her palms.

Ow! Hat protested as he bumped into the roof of the tunnel.

Sorry. Julie ducked her head and glanced back at Cassidy, who was inches behind her. Taylor had put out the flame, and Cassidy's red eyes glowed eerily in the dark. *You know, Hat, I never thought I'd say this, but I'm nostalgic for the Brooklyn sewers.*

Same. Hat sighed.

"Blood," Cassidy hissed from very close behind Julie. "I smell blood."

"Quiet!" Isaiah whispered. The wolf was down on his belly, and past him, Julie could see a shimmer of pale-blue light at the end of the tunnel. The light looked familiar, and snowflakes drifted in it.

"That looks like what we saw in the sewers before they closed the portal," Taylor murmured.

Julie nodded.

Isaiah came to a stop. "We're here."

CHAPTER SEVEN

Julie crawled up beside Isaiah, his doggy smell filling her nose. Peering past him, she looked into a huge cavern jagged with stalagmites and stalactites. Snow drifted against the walls, filtering in through the crack in the high ceiling through which the soft blue light was shining. It was sunlight, Julie realized, but distant and filtered by ice and snow.

The floor was covered with Yetis.

They were everywhere, their shaggy black coats speckled with snow and their massive forms eerily still as they stood in silent ranks all over the floor. None stirred. Their huge hands hung down by their sides, ending in blunt nails, and their tusks jutted from lower jaws set in expressionless faces. In front, a gigantic Yeti stood impassive, tufts of gray hair on either side of its head marking it as one of the elders.

It's like they've been switched off, Julie thought. *Are they hibernating?*

Hibernating? Winter is a Yeti's element, Hat told her. *This isn't normal.*

Cassidy clutched Julie's arm, and her claws dug into Julie's skin. "There," the vampire hissed, pointing at a tall, icy passageway leading out of the cavern on the other side of the Yetis. "Malcolm's through there."

"Can we sneak around them?" Julie whispered.

Beside her, Isaiah shook his head. "There's only one way to that cavern. Through the Yetis."

The other werewolves yipped in anticipation. Julie looked over her shoulder. Taylor had his staff in one hand and his sheathed sword in the other. When their eyes met, the elf nodded.

"Okay." Julie sighed. "Let's do this."

Hat's warmth disappeared, and the soft wool over Julie's ears turned to metal. A nose guard crept down the bridge of her nose, and cold iron wrapped around her cheeks.

She looked at Cassidy, who was still painfully clutching her arm. "Hey, you know how you are batshit-crazy sometimes?"

Cassidy glared at her. "Excuse me?"

"This would be a good time for that." Julie gestured at the Yetis. "Have at 'em."

A grin crossed Cassidy's face, and her fangs grew. She let out a shrieking, inhuman cry that raised goosebumps across Julie's skin.

"*Malcolm!*" Cassidy screamed, then launched out of the tunnel and down the long incline toward the Yetis.

"Charge!" Julie yelled, flinging herself through the mouth of the tunnel. "I'll cover you!"

The werewolves barreled forward with a melodic chorus of snarls and howls, close on Cassidy's heels.

As one, the Yetis reanimated. The gray-tufted elder reared back, its eyes snapping wide, and let out a gargling, Wookie-like roar. The others surged forward to meet Cassidy and the Weres.

A blast of blue fire rushed past Julie and hit one of the charging Yetis in the chest. It tumbled backward, roaring, and rolled to put out the fire.

"Shoot, Julie!" Taylor yelled. "*Shoot!*"

Julie trained her sights on a charging Yeti and squeezed the trigger slowly. She hovered at a couple of pounds of pressure, following the moving target as it barreled toward Isaiah.

"Julie!" Taylor sent a sweeping arc of blue fire toward the Yetis.

They're mind-controlled. This isn't right, Julie told Hat.

Magic crackled through her gun. *I've set it to stun. Shoot!* Hat yelled.

Julie pulled the trigger, and a crackling ball of electricity launched from the barrel and slammed into the Yeti's chest. The creature tumbled headlong to the ground, inches from Isaiah's forepaws. The golden werewolf leaped at the next attacker, fangs bared. He landed on its chest and bowled it over, snapping at its throat.

Cassidy and the other Weres slammed into the front lines of the Yetis. Taylor tucked the shrunken staff behind his ear and drew his sword, then charged with a defiant yell. Julie kept firing into the ranks of Yetis behind the seething mass of violence at the front. The Yetis had become a close-packed swarm pushing against her hopelessly outnumbered friends. Gaps opened in the swarm as Julie's shots found their targets.

A yelping scream filled the air. One of the Yetis had seized Noah by a front and hind leg and raised him into the air, and the little wolf was squealing and clawing at the air. Blood seeped into the werewolf's fur where the Yeti's nails had ripped the skin.

"Noah!" Julie screamed and took aim, but they were moving too fast. She wasn't sure she could hit the Yeti instead of the Were.

Taylor's yell split the air, and his blade flashed among the mass of Yetis. One fell at his feet and he moved forward, his feet dancing across the rocky floor and his sword coming around in a shimmering arc. It slashed into the Yeti's ribs, and the creature fell without a sound. Noah tumbled to the ground, then rolled to his feet and gave Taylor a brief nod before plunging back into the fray.

Julie's hands were shaking. *That Yeti was ready to smash Noah against the ground. It would have killed him.*

They're fighting to kill, Hat agreed.

Julie looked at her gun. The Yetis she'd shot were still lying motionless. She fired into the fray again, avoiding the place where Cassidy had become a blur of chaos. Yetis fell left and right as she concentrated her fire on the ones around the scattered Weres. Her friends were being driven back toward the tunnel they had entered through. Only the whirlwind that was Cassidy was holding her ground. When Julie glanced toward her, the vampire flung a full-grown Yeti across the room, taking down a swathe of others charging toward Isaiah.

It wasn't enough; Isaiah was swarmed. Two Yetis grabbed his hind legs, and others snatched for his throat. He spun this way and that, hackles rippling, snapping in all directions. Julie fired at the two clutching his legs and they fell, but the golden wolf was surrounded again.

Taylor's scream ripped her attention from Isaiah, and her heart stuttered in her chest. A Yeti had him by the throat, giant hands locked around his neck, and was lifting him into the air. Taylor's legs kicked helplessly and his hands scrabbled at the Yeti's forearms, clawing for its face, but its arms were too long. He was helpless.

Another Yeti approached, hands outstretched, its gargling cry filled with menace. They were going to tear him limb from limb. Taylor's kicking slowed, and his head lolled in the Yeti's grasp.

Julie fired. The first projectile took down the charging Yeti, and the second slammed into the chest of the one holding Taylor. It crumpled to the ground, and Taylor fell with a sickening thump, then lay unmoving.

"Shit! *Taylor!*" Julie's hands shook on her gun.

The Weres were fighting hard, alone and outnumbered. Three

Yetis charged at Taylor's limp form. She ran toward him and shot two of them, but more came faster than she could fire. Three more fell, and when the fourth reached Taylor, Julie got there first. She swung the gun with all her strength, and its barrel cracked across the Yeti's face with a force that sent it to the ground.

"Taylor!" Julie grabbed the front of his jacket and shook him.

"Hmm?" Taylor's eyelids flickered, to her relief.

The smell of wet dog filled the air as Austin thundered past her, his brown fur streaked with blood. "Get him out of here!" the werewolf shouted before crashing into the oncoming mass of Yetis.

Julie kept her gun in one hand, holding it up as she gave Taylor a brief slap on one cheek. "Wake up!"

The elf stirred, limbs twitching. "Wha…"

Julie grabbed his arm and hauled it over her shoulders. "Come on, Taylor. Come *on!*"

The elf fumbled to his feet, his weight dragging at Julie's shoulders. She shot an oncoming Yeti and stumbled toward the tunnel, Taylor leaning heavily against her. Her lungs were burning and her legs were wobbly when they reached the mouth of the tunnel and she could let Taylor go. He swayed, then leaned against the wall, but he stayed on his feet.

"Are you okay?" Julie eyed the reddening marks on his throat.

Taylor touched them and shook his head. His eyes were clearing, but his voice was hoarse and raw when he spoke. "I'm okay." He looked toward the fight, and his face fell. "Julie, we're not winning."

Blake had broken free of the fray. Ears pricked toward the passage on the far side, the werewolf ran toward it in a broad arc. Three Yetis broke off from the intense fight around Cassidy, leaving their kin to struggle as they rushed at Blake and brought him to bay against the wall, fighting for his life.

"We've got to do something," Julie insisted.

"I'm out of ideas." Taylor cleared his throat. "Should we pull back?"

He's weakening. Cassidy's words came back to Julie, and her stomach clenched. "We can't leave Malcolm," she murmured, her eyes darting to the sharp stalactite in front of her. They were everywhere, hanging ominously over the cavern.

"I know that face. That's your idea face." Taylor straightened. "Tell me it's a good one."

"Hat, can you make it so I can speak telepathically into everyone's minds?" Julie demanded.

"Yes." Hat hummed busily for a moment. "Okay. You're linked."

Julie took a deep breath, hoping that this would work. *Hey! Everyone!*

The Weres hesitated, then glanced toward her as they fought. Even Cassidy had slowed down. The vampire was hissing as two Yetis circled her. She had streaks of blood on her cheeks and a bruise reddening on her jaw.

We're not fighting as a team. We can beat this if we work together! Julie called into their minds.

How? Isaiah replied in her mind, thanks to Hat.

I have a plan. We need to pull back toward the tunnel. Everyone! Julie called into their minds. *Make them think they've won.*

Isaiah was silent, and Cassidy's red eyes met hers across the cavern. *Okay.*

Julie raised the gun in her shaking hands. "Hat, I need you to set this thing to the most destructive ammo it's got. Something that explodes."

"Done," Hat told her.

Taylor bent to pick up his staff.

Julie sucked in a breath and aimed at the largest stalactite in the cavern. It hung over the center of the room, its sharp tip gleaming in the sunlight.

Now! she cried.

Yelping and squealing, the werewolves broke free of the battle and fled toward the tunnel. Noah limped as he ran. Cassidy overtook them in seconds. As one, the Yetis pursued them.

Julie waited until Noah was clear of the last Yeti, then fired.

The gun kicked like a carthorse and slammed her into the wall as something improbably huge and flaming hurtled from the muzzle. Julie's breath hitched, but her aim was true. The ball of fire struck the stalactite at the base, and with a creaking rumble, it cracked.

The gray-tufted elder let out a high-pitched warble. The Yetis all skidded to a halt and looked up as the stalactite juddered, swayed, and then fell.

Roars of panic filled the cavern as the stalactite thundered to the ground, then dust and shards of ice exploded in all directions. The Yetis scattered, their ranks broken.

"Now!" Julie screamed. "Weres, Cassidy, charge! Taylor, we'll follow and cover them!"

In a tight-knit pack, they lunged forward, dodging still-skidding bits of rock and ice as they skirted around the rubble of the fallen stalactite where the group of Yetis was at its thinnest. Disoriented, the creatures barely seemed to notice the approaching Weres before Julie raised her gun—set to stun again —and fired into the chest of the nearest one. It fell without a sound, and its companion whipped around just in time for Isaiah's leap to tackle it to the ground.

Bellows of rage echoed around Julie, and the Yetis charged, but there were only a few yards to go before they reached the passageway that led to Malcolm. "Keep going!" Julie yelled, then swung hard to the left and fired two shots. Blue fire flared on her right. Cassidy flitted this way and that, biting and clawing. The Weres snapped, snarled, and punched their way through the Yetis.

"Behind you!" Hat yelled.

Julie whipped around with barely enough time to fire a ball of electricity into the chest of a Yeti feet away from her. The creature fell at her feet, and a flare of blue fire rushed past her face, catching another Yeti's coat as it lunged at her. Julie ducked the falling, yowling, burning Yeti and fired to her right, shooting the one that was about to grab Taylor.

Noah fell to the ground, yelping. Two Yetis were tearing out chunks of his fur. Immediately, Blake and Cassidy were on them, snapping and shrieking. One of the Yetis reared back, Cassidy's fangs embedded in its throat, and clawed at her with a gargling scream. Blake and the other Yeti tumbled out of the way, and Julie ran to Noah. He was in his human form, curled in a ball, blood seeping through the rips in his blue uniform.

"Stop!" Hat cried.

Julie tried, but she was running too fast. The Yeti that lunged at her feet succeeded in knocking them out from under her, sending her hard to the ground. Her elbow slammed into the unforgiving rock with stabbing pain. Her gun skidded out of her hands, and Julie snatched at it a second too late. Her fingertips slid across the metal as the Yeti seized her by the calves and yanked her back.

She rolled over, kicking and shrieking, as the monstrous creature straddled her. Its massive weight pinned her to the ground, and its giant hands closed around her throat. She heard Taylor yell her name and felt a bolt of panic, but the hands on her throat sparked a memory in her muscles. In a sweeping movement, Julie brought both hands up and together between the Yeti's forearms, breaking its grip as she raised her hips, twisting them to knock the creature off-balance. It pitched toward her, and she threw her arms around its neck, pinning it against her shoulder. Its ear came invitingly within reach, and she sank her teeth into it.

The Yeti screeched in pain and indignation, then shoved her away and rolled off her. She threw herself on her belly and crawled desperately for her gun. She grabbed it and flipped onto her back as the creature lunged, firing a stun ball into its chest.

The Yeti shrieked and fell face-first at her feet.

Taylor struggled free of the Yeti that was trying to strangle him, sent a blast of blue fire into its chest, and ran over to Julie. She was already on her feet. "We have to keep going! Get Noah!"

"We're there. We're there!" Taylor panted.

Julie whipped around. Blake and Cassidy were carrying the semi-conscious Noah into the passage just feet away while the other Weres held off the tide of Yetis.

"Come on!" she yelled. "We're nearly there!"

She raised her gun and shot three Yetis in quick succession, allowing the Weres to back up toward the passageway. After a few more bursts of blue fire from Taylor, they were inside the passage. A Yeti immediately tried to push through after them, and Taylor lunged with his staff, filling the entire opening with a wall of blue flame. There were roars and screams from beyond.

Sweat coursed down Julie's forehead. Or maybe it was blood. She didn't think so. She dragged her forearm over her face and turned to the rest of the battered little group, all of them pale and sweating and breathless. Noah slumped against the wall of the passageway, ashen but breathing and whimpering as he clutched an obviously broken wrist to his chest.

Cassidy's eyes were two red flames in the dim passage. "This way!" She turned and bolted along it.

Isaiah stood up from where he'd been crouched beside Noah. "We'll hold them off. It'll be easy in this small space." He glanced at Noah, his eyes hardening. "I won't let them get through. You go get your friend."

Taylor held out the staff. "Here. It's pre-charged with blue fire, so you'll be able to use it."

Isaiah shook his head with a barking laugh. "I've got fangs and claws for that. You go. Quick!"

It ripped Julie's heart to leave the Weres behind, but he was right. "Come on!" She grabbed Taylor's sleeve, and they ran after Cassidy.

The passage twisted twice before opening up into a whole new cavern. Cassidy was standing in the opening, her chest heaving, her clawed hands curled into fists.

"Malcolllmm," she hissed.

CHAPTER EIGHT

"Shhh!" Julie reached up and clapped a hand over Cassidy's mouth, dragging her back. "They haven't seen us!"

The vampire resisted for a split second, then calmed and allowed Julie to drag her to the ground behind the cover of one of several large cardboard boxes dumped willy-nilly around the outside of the cavern. Cautiously, Julie raised her head and peered over the box.

The space was much smaller than the previous one, and, apart from the abandoned boxes, it was meticulously laid out. Portable laboratory lamps on tripods, spaced around the perimeter of the cavern, provided an eerie yellow light. Devices Julie didn't recognize—scientific-looking things, glass and plastic and metal—filled the center of the room. A chalk circle was surrounded by candles and runes. Their dim flames burned with creepy stillness in the motionless air of the cavern.

Julie was staring so hard at the circle that it took her a moment to notice the movement at the back of the room. A figure in a white lab coat lay on the ground. Julie caught a glimpse of a green-skinned cheek and a blonde ponytail.

"Qtana!" she whispered. The person standing over her, also wearing a white coat, was another troll.

Cassidy quietly rose beside her, trembling uncontrollably with the force of trying to hold back her Quickening. The vampire pointed with a deadly claw. "There he is."

Beside the trolls was a tall cage, its ornate bars gleaming silver. A slumped, slender form lay on the bottom of it.

Julie's heart squeezed in her chest. "Malcolm," she whispered. She looked at Taylor. "Okay, what's the plan? What does the circle do?"

"It's some kind of dark and powerful magic," Taylor murmured, shuddering. "If we can damage the circle, it will be broken."

"Portal magic?" Julie asked.

Taylor shook his head. "Something stronger."

She swallowed, nodding. "Okay, so we need to distract the trolls while—"

Cassidy let out a strangled cry.

"Cassidy, no!" Julie gasped.

It was too late. The vampire vaulted over the cardboard box and darted around the perimeter of the room with a shrieking hiss. The upright troll whipped around, and Julie recognized his hard eyes.

"Qbiit?" she gasped.

Qbiit yanked a pistol from under his lab coat and aimed it at Cassidy. Julie fired too quickly, and the ball of electricity flew wide and pinged off a table, then scorched a black spot on the wall. Qbiit whirled and aimed his pistol at her instead. Two shots cracked through the air, and dust exploded from the wall above her head.

"Malcolm!" Cassidy screeched.

Julie peered over the box. Cassidy had reached the cage and she lunged, grabbing the bars with both hands. There was a sizzling crackle like an electrical short, and Cassidy was thrown to the floor.

"No!" Taylor yelled.

A blast of blue fire arced over Julie's head and slammed into the cardboard box nearest Qbiit. The troll squealed, holstered his weapon, and grabbed a fire extinguisher from a nearby table. It spat a greenish foam that seemed to work on the blue flames, but they had distracted him.

"Get Cassidy and Malcolm!" Julie barked. "I'll grab Qtana!"

Taylor nodded once, then scrambled out from behind the box and ran across the floor. Qbiit whirled to face him and Julie stepped forward, cocking her gun.

"Don't move!" she yelled.

Qbiit froze, the extinguisher still in his hands. He reached for his pistol, and Julie gestured sharply with hers. "I told you not to move!" *Hat,* she added silently, *set it to kill.* Her eyes darted to Taylor, who was crouching beside Cassidy. If it was Qbiit or Taylor, she was sure who she'd save.

Done, Hat growled. *Try to get him to talk while you sneak over and destroy the circle. This magic is evil. Old and evil.*

"What are you doing here, human?" Qbiit hissed. "None of this concerns you."

"Oh, you think?" Julie snorted.

"This is paranormal business." Qbiit's eyes darted from Julie to the chalk circle.

Julie took another step forward, and the troll flinched. "You've hurt my friends. That makes it my business." Her voice rang through the cavern.

Qbiit's eyes narrowed. "Stay out of this. You all should have stayed out of this." He glared at Qtana's motionless form.

"Why did you take Malcolm?" Julie shot back. "What did you want with him?"

Qbiit sneered. "He came too close, and he had something I needed."

"Needed for what, Qbiit?" Julie inclined her head, indicating the circle. "What is this?"

Qbiit smiled, the shadows from the candles elongating on his face. "Nothing a simple human would understand."

Julie took another step. "Try me."

Taylor fell to his knees beside Cassidy. The vampire lay on her back, eyes closed, her burned hands clutched to her chest. "Cassidy! Cassidy, come *on*!" He shrank the staff and tucked it behind his ear, then glanced at the trolls. Julie was keeping Qbiit talking, her gun still trained on his chest.

Cassidy stirred. "Mmm?"

Taylor shook her shoulders. "Wake up!"

Cassidy sat bolt upright with a ragged gasp. "Malcolm!" she whimpered. Her eyes were a paler red, and tears welled in them.

"Stay right here!" Taylor ordered. He rose and hurried to the cage. Malcolm lay on his back, one arm flung out to the side like he'd been dragged there. His Assassin's Creed T-shirt and sweatpants were smudged with dirt and blood. His face was deathly pale, and blue veins traced across his cheeks. His chest rose and fell in short, shallow breaths.

The silver was poisoning him.

"Hang on, Malcolm!" Taylor wrapped a hand around the heavy lock that held the door and closed his eyes, feeling the mechanisms within. Whatever Qbiit had done with the chalk circle, the troll didn't have magic, and this wasn't a magic lock. The lock clicked open, and Taylor yanked the door wide and rushed inside to grasp Malcolm's arms. The vampire's head lolled back lifelessly as Taylor tried to pull him upright.

"Malcolm!" Cassidy sobbed.

"It's okay!" Taylor called, his words covered by Julie's and Qbiit's yelling. In the passage, he thought he heard the Weres barking and the snarls of the Yetis, but there was no time to worry about that. Whatever he'd just said, Malcolm was *not* okay.

He hauled the limp vampire over his shoulder and carried him out of the cage.

Cassidy was sitting up, and she extended her burned hands to Taylor, tears streaking her pale face. Taylor glanced over his shoulder at Qbiit. The troll was still yelling at Julie.

"We need to get him out of here." Taylor reached for Cassidy's arm.

She dodged him. "He's dying. Please put him down. He needs blood."

Taylor's heart faltered. *Dying?*

"Please," Cassidy sobbed.

Taylor crouched and gently lowered Malcolm to the floor. The vampire was barely breathing. Cassidy struggled to swallow her tears and held out her forearm, raising her claws. Before Taylor could stop her, she slashed her skin, opening a long red wound that oozed scarlet blood.

"Come on, my love. Please, keep fighting," Cassidy cried. Tears and blood dripped onto Malcolm's chest as Cassidy leaned forward, holding her wounded arm against Malcolm's half-open mouth. Blood dripped onto his lips.

Taylor glanced at Qbiit again. "We have to hurry."

Qbiit's eyes narrowed as Julie took another step toward the chalk circle. "Don't come any closer!" he hissed.

"Are you forgetting which one of us is holding the gun?" Julie spat. "You didn't answer my question. What *is* all this?"

Qbiit bared his yellowed teeth in a snarl. "This is some of the greatest magic the world has ever seen. Magic that most are too cowardly to touch!"

Funny he should say that considering that trolls are completely unmagical, Hat scoffed.

Julie frowned. "Trolls don't have magic. That's why you're

stuck in IT."

Qbiit's eyes flashed. "Shut up, human!" he yelled. "You're just like everyone else. Stupid troll, ugly troll, non-magical troll, nasty, bad, scary troll!" His hands clenched on the fire extinguisher he was still holding. "I'll show the world that trolls were made for more than IT. I'll show them that there's more to politics than the seven royal families. I'll show them!"

"Stop!" Julie yelled as Qbiit raised the fire extinguisher and held it over Qtana's motionless form. Her finger hovered on the trigger.

"Shoot me, and this falls on her face," Qbiit snarled. "Stay away from that circle."

"Drop that, and I'll drop *you*," Julie snapped. "Put the extinguisher down, and we'll all walk away from this."

Tell him you'll take him back to HQ, and we'll figure it out there, Hat suggested.

Julie nodded. "Let's go back to HQ and get all this straightened out."

"Straightened out?" Qbiit cackled. "*Straightened out?* This is so much bigger than you can ever dream, human."

Try to get him to tell you who he's working for, Hat prompted.

"Why don't you enlighten me?" Julie glanced at the cage. It was empty, and she could see Taylor and Cassidy crouching over a bleeding Malcolm. Taylor's sword was in his hand. "Who are you working for, Qbiit? You didn't do all this magic yourself."

Qbiit let out a guttural roar of anger and raised the extinguisher.

"Don't!" Julie took aim.

At Qbiit's feet, Qtana stirred, raising her blood-soaked ponytail from the floor. "What's happening?"

———

Malcolm finally stirred. Letting out a moan, he grasped Cassidy's arm and pulled it close, sucking the blood from her wound.

Taylor tried to ignore how gross that was and focused on the color that was returning to Malcolm's cheeks. He put a hand on the vampire's shoulder and gave him a little shake. "Hey, Malcolm? You with us yet?"

Malcolm let go of Cassidy's arm, and his eyes flickered open. Their normal red was nearly pink. "Wh...what happened?" he croaked.

"Oh, Malcolm!" Cassidy pulled him close and clung to him.

Malcolm groaned but managed to wrap an arm around Cassidy.

Taylor glanced at the trolls, and his stomach clenched. Qtana was trying to get to her knees. Qbiit held a fire extinguisher threateningly over her head, and Julie was holding her gun at the ready. The barks and howls from the passageway were getting louder.

Closer.

"Take care of Malcolm. Get him out of here," Taylor barked at Cassidy as he drew his sword.

"Qtana, look out!" Julie yelled.

The blonde troll had struggled to her hands and knees, and Qbiit whirled, raising the fire extinguisher in a threatening motion. Julie fired, but the shot missed by inches, instead punching a hole in the rock wall. She rushed forward, but as she reached the chalk circle, it began to glow bright red.

Look out! Hat cried.

Julie skidded to a halt, feeling the sting of magic in the air. There was a deafening roar from the passageway. Weres and Yetis spilled into the cavern, snarling and fighting, fur and saliva flying. Julie threw herself behind one of the science-y things as

Isaiah and Blake tumbled past, fighting tooth and nail.

Qtana screamed. Julie scrabbled to her knees and raised the gun as Qbiit swung the extinguisher.

Qtana threw herself to the floor.

The metal narrowly missed her head, but Qbiit gathered himself for another swing. He drove the extinguisher toward Qtana's face…and metal rang on metal as Taylor's blade blocked the blow. Keeping both hands on the extinguisher, Qbiit yelped and looked up. Taylor slapped him across the face, the smacking blow sending the troll stumbling backward. The extinguisher fell to the floor, and Julie took aim again.

No! Stop! Hat gasped. *This cavern is filled with Weres. If it ricochets—*

"Shit!" Julie hissed.

Taylor strode forward, his sword a whirlwind of steel, and Qbiit was driven back to the wall.

"Put up your hands!" Taylor growled, pointing the sword at Qbiit's face. He was so focused on the troll that he didn't notice the Yeti launch at him from behind.

Julie's gun crackled with magic. *Fire!* Hat shrieked.

"Taylor, look out!" Julie screamed as she pulled the trigger. A ball of electricity crackled from the muzzle but slammed into the Yeti a second too late. The creature's full weight crashed into Taylor, and they fell to the floor in a messy heap. Taylor's sword flew from his hand, skidded across the ground with a metallic clink, and came to rest a few inches from Julie.

She grabbed the hilt.

You don't know how to swordfight! Hat protested.

Julie weighed the blade in her hands. *It's time I learned.*

Taylor scrambled to his feet, shoving the stunned Yeti off him. Blood flowed from a cut lip. Julie rushed forward. The elf was already reaching behind his ear for the staff.

"I don't think so," Qbiit snarled.

Julie's stomach flipped as she skidded to a halt beside Taylor.

Snarls and snaps filled the room as the Weres struggled to hold the Yetis away from Taylor and Julie. Qbiit's mouth twisted in a grin. He was holding the staff, blue fire crackling around its tip.

You have a clear shot. Take it! Hat cried.

Qbiit reached down with his free hand and grabbed Qtana by her hair, wrenching the injured troll to her feet. She let out a scream of agony as Qbiit held her in front of him as a shield. "No, little human," he snarled. "I don't think so."

There! On the table to your left! The tray! Hat yelped. *It's obsidian. It'll work as a shield!*

Julie shoved Taylor's sword into his hands and grabbed the tray, scattering syringes filled with what she could only assume was vampire blood as blue fire roared from the staff's tip. She threw the tray up with a scream, waiting for her skin to burn, but the stone stayed cool in her hands as the fire bounced off it.

She peered over the top of her makeshift shield. Qbiit snarled at her. He was keeping Qtana's head near his shoulder, his staff still aimed. Her hand went to her gun, but there was no way to shoot with Qtana in front of him.

Taylor flexed his fingers on the hilt of his sword, ready to attack. Qbiit's eyes slid to him, and Julie stepped forward as if to rush him. "*Hey!* Over here, you ugly troll!"

Qbiit turned to her and sent a blast of fire arcing her way. Julie ducked behind her shield, and flames licked its edges as she waited out the blast of fire. When she looked up again, Taylor's eyes met hers. He'd crept a few feet closer while Qbiit was blasting her. He gave her the faintest of nods, which she returned.

"That all you've got, you stupid troll?" she called. "Not so magical when you only have a pre-charged staff, are you?"

Qbiit roared and blasted fire again, hotter and longer this time. Julie gritted her teeth as she darted behind a table that had been upturned in the fight with the Yetis, then held up the shield over her head. She glanced over her shoulder at the glowing red circle, but the Yetis had formed a defensive ring around it, keeping the Weres back. Noah was still in the passage, his face ashen, and blood ran from cuts on Isaiah's flanks. All the Weres were panting and trembling, their strength spent.

The fire winked out. Julie stood up, laughing. "Kinda pathetic, huh? I mean, you can't even handle a single helpless human."

"Shut up!" Qbiit shrieked. Flames flared around the staff.

"C'mon, Qbiit. You've got to see how sad it is that you had no idea that my taunting was just a diversion, you crazy *bitch*!" Julie yelled.

Taylor lunged. Snatching Qtana's arm with one hand, he wrenched her away from Qbiit as he brought his sword around in a shining arc. The troll leaped back, crying out as the blade ripped through the sleeve of his coat. Red blood stained the white fabric. Qtana fell against Taylor and he stumbled back, his balance lost. The troll clutched at him, slowing his sword arm for a crucial second.

"*NO!*" Qbiit howled, whirling and raising the staff.

"Taylor!" Julie shrieked.

Taylor let out a yell and spun, shielding Qtana with his body. Blue flames roared toward him, blazing across the back of his jacket. Julie launched from behind the table and tackled Qbiit, and the blue fire winked out when the staff left his hand. Julie kicked away from the troll and slithered across the ground to grab the staff, then rolled onto her back to aim it at Qbiit.

"Yetis! Yetis! To me!" Qbiit screamed.

Three Yetis launched at Julie. She held up the staff, felt Hat hum with magic, and sent blue flames into the oncoming creatures. Taylor was suddenly beside her, his sword in his hands, panting with pain as smoke rose from his ruined jacket.

They backed against the wall. Julie glanced over her shoulder to see Qtana stumbling over to where Malcolm lay on the floor. Cassidy stood over them both, fangs and claws ready to protect.

She sent another blast of fire at the Yetis. "Taylor, your shoulder."

The elf glanced at the nasty burn extending over the skin. "It's okay. It's fixable. I just can't use it."

Julie spun the staff and launched fire at a Yeti, but another charged her. "I'll cover your left side. You cover my right. We fight through the Yetis, and we get to the circle."

She's right, Hat interjected. *If we break the circle, the Yetis will be free.*

Taylor nodded. "Go."

They stepped forward, shoulder to shoulder, and Julie sent an arc of fire into the approaching Yetis. As the staff recharged, Taylor swung his sword, opening a gash on a charging Yeti's chest.

Four o'clock! Hat barked. Julie fired the staff behind Taylor's back. A Yeti stumbled backward, roaring, as fire flared across its fur.

Weres! Hat shouted. *Weres, to our flanks!*

Isaiah let out a hoarse, breathless howl, and the Weres pushed through the Yetis toward Julie and Taylor. The fighting wolves flanked them, and they drove like a wedge toward the circle.

"Stop them! Stop them!" Qbiit squealed.

The Yetis pushed back. One of them snatched at Julie's staff, and her shoulders were wrenched as it tried to haul the staff away from her. Taylor slashed at its forearms, and it stumbled back, squealing.

Behind you! Hat called. Julie fired flames into the face of a Yeti that was about to grab Taylor. Beside her, Austin locked his jaws on a Yeti's leg, drawing a screech from it. It snatched at him, and Blake reared up and snapped at its arms.

Only one Yeti remained between Julie and the circle, its black fur backlit by the crimson glow.

Charge! Charge now! Hat cried. With a yell, Julie rushed at it, blasting fire and feinting to the left. The Yeti dodged the fire and lunged to the left. Julie threw herself to the right instead, ducking under her blue flames.

The Yeti let out a roar. Julie lunged for the chalk circle with her staff, but the creature's huge foot thundered into her ribs and sent her skidding across the floor. Darkness popped in front of her eyes, her breath driven from her.

Pain blossomed through Julie's ribs. She curled around them, wheezing, desperate for air and conscious of the Yeti lumbering toward her while her staff lay a few feet away. Taylor was slashing at the three Yetis surrounding him. Julie reached for the staff, and the Yeti kicked it toward Taylor.

"Tay—" Julie wheezed, but before she could scream his name, the Yeti planted a gigantic foot on her chest and pressed down. Her ribs cracked. She tried to breathe, but her chest wouldn't lift, and her lungs burned for air.

Julie, kick him in the shin! Hat shouted. *Now!*

Julie didn't think she had the strength. The Yeti pressed harder and her mouth fell open, but no air would come. Her vision blurred. The world felt very far away.

Julie! Hat wailed.

Julie summoned the last of her strength and kicked, and the blow struck the Yeti's shin. Its foot on her chest lifted a fraction.

Now, Taylor! Hat shouted.

Taylor slammed his blade into a Yeti's foot. The creature reared back, screaming, and Taylor made a flicking motion toward the staff. It sailed through the air and landed in Julie's hand.

She reached for the glowing circle and thrust the head of the staff through the chalk.

The circle was broken.

The glow winked out, and the angry roars in the cavern cut off.

"*Nooooooooo!*" Qbiit screamed.

The Yeti stepped back, and Julie sucked in a glorious breath of air, then rolled to her feet. She aimed the staff at the creature, but it was staring at her, wide-eyed and silent. Not a single Yeti moved. They blinked at each other and at Julie, then at Taylor and the Weres, who stood panting in a tight group. Taylor still held his sword, but no one attacked.

Qbiit reared up from behind the table he'd used as cover. "Fight them! Fight them, you idiots!"

The gray-tufted Yeti fixed its eyes on Qbiit, then looked at the circle. It let out a roar that shook the walls of the cavern, then bolted back down the passage, ignoring Noah. The other Yetis followed.

Everyone in the cavern turned to look at Qbiit.

The troll let out a gargling shriek. Seizing one of the vampire-blood-filled syringes, he rushed at Julie, raising it over his head like a javelin. She stepped aside and stuck out a foot. Qbiit tripped and sprawled on the floor.

"Seriously, dude?" Julie poked him with a toe. "How was that supposed to work out for you?"

Taylor clapped the magical handcuffs on the troll and hauled him to his feet.

"You don't understand," Qbiit spat. "You don't know what you're meddling with!"

"Yeah, yeah. Save it for your trial." Taylor dragged him toward the passage, screaming, and Malcolm, Noah, and Qtana, supported by the other Weres and Cassidy, followed.

CHAPTER NINE

When Genevieve purred through the gates of the PMA, Julie's foot stuttered on the accelerator for a moment. "What's all this?"

Hat chuckled from his seat on the dashboard. "Looks like a hero's welcome to me."

Isaiah plastered himself against the passenger window, gaping. "Are we heroes now?"

The drive leading to the front doors of the HQ building was lined with people. Uniforms of all colors—plenty of green this time, Julie noted—shone in the golden evening light. No one cheered, but they all stared as Julie brought Genevieve to a halt outside the doors. Cassidy's Porsche and Taylor's Mitsubishi flanked the gleaming pewter Mustang.

Julie stepped out of the car, smirking. Isaiah followed. He was suitably battle-scarred, as well as being sweaty and muscular, and the younger female paras in the crowd murmured in admiration. A few of them waved. Isaiah waved back.

"Not bad. You're only three days into training and already a hero, huh?" Julie quipped.

Isaiah gave her a sheepish smile. "May I go to the ER now, miss? I want to see if Noah is okay."

OPMA medics had arrived via portal to take Noah and Qtana to the ER in Central Park. Julie nodded. "Go on. You need some attention too."

Isaiah jogged off, followed by the other Weres as they piled out of their transports, and Julie turned to the Mitsubishi. Wincing as he moved, Taylor opened the back door. He grabbed Qbiit by the arm and hauled the handcuffed troll into the sunlight.

A gasp rippled through the crowd, followed by a cheer when Malcolm climbed out of the passenger seat of Cassidy's Porsche, pale and leaning heavily on his fiancée.

"Book him, Danno," Julie quipped.

Taylor stared at her. "What?"

"Never mind. Let's get this sucker into the containment unit." Julie marched up the steps to the doors, followed by the others. Inside the entrance hall, there was an even bigger crowd of people lining the hall.

Should I wave like the Queen? she wondered.

Don't push it, Hat cautioned.

Julie smiled at a few people for good measure, then focused on the end of the hall. Kaplan was waiting, arms folded, jaw jutting, amber eyes unreadable. Julius Nox stood beside him.

The doors banged shut behind Malcolm and Cassidy.

"My *son!*" Julius cried. He ran down the hall, dignity abandoned and his disheveled black hair in a cloud behind him. Reaching Malcolm, he threw his arms around the injured young vampire and hugged him.

"Sire. *Sire!*" Malcolm grumbled.

Julius held the embrace for a few more seconds before stepping back. His eyes were damp. "Oh, Malcolm. I'm so glad you're all right."

"He needs more blood." Cassidy kept a hand on Malcolm's arm. "He was exposed to silver."

"Silver!" Julius turned, and when his eyes rested on Qbiit, they glowed in a way that made Cassidy in full Quickening mode seem as harmless as a baby bunny. Julie felt a chill slither down her spine. The vampire glared for a moment before turning to Julie. "Miss Meadows, you did it."

"*We* did it, Sire." Julie gestured at Taylor and Cassidy and added, "The Weres, too."

Julius wrung Taylor's hand, then Julie's. His grip was ice-cold, and his words were strangled. "Thank you." He took Malcolm's arm. "Let's get you to the medical unit."

Three agents stepped forward, grabbed Qbiit, and roughly hustled the troll down the hall toward the elevator. Kaplan stepped aside to let him go, but as Qbiit passed him, he uttered a growl that was barely audible but shook the floor. Qbiit's greenish skin turned white, and Julie felt a pang of satisfaction.

"I look forward to your trial, troll," Kaplan rumbled.

Qbiit hung his head. The agents dragged him to the elevator, and Kaplan turned to face Julie and Taylor. His eyes dwelled on them just long enough for him to nod, then he strode after the agents and Qbiit.

"Um, Julie?"

Cassidy was wringing her hands. Her eyes were back to their usual deep scarlet, and she had neatly manicured nails on her hands, but there were blood and bruises on her face.

Julie summoned a smile. "Glad to see you're feeling better."

"Listen, I treated you really badly before." Cassidy's eyes dropped to the floor. "I was speciesist, and there's no excuse for that. I'd like to blame the Quickening, but let's be real." She spread her hands. "I'm a crazy psycho bitch at times."

"Hey, all the best people are." Julie grinned. "You were awesome in there, even with the Quickening to deal with."

Cassidy hooked her hair behind her ear, and a faint smile touched her lips. "Can I ask you something?"

"Sure."

Hesitantly, Cassidy gripped Julie's hands. "Malcolm wouldn't be here if it wasn't for you. Both of you." She glanced at Taylor. "Would you be the guests of honor at our handfasting?"

Julie beamed. "Absolutely!"

"Great!" A real smile blossomed on Cassidy's face for the first time Julie could remember. The vampire wrapped her in a brief cold hug. "Thank you!"

Julie barely had time to return the embrace before Cassidy trotted out the door after Malcolm and Julius. "Hey, Taylor. How did she know you were my plus-one?"

"It must be our amazing chemistry," Taylor snarked. "Or maybe Mal—" His face twisted, and he clasped his injured arm to his side with his free hand, gritting his teeth.

"Okay, enough standing around talking." Julie gripped his arm. "Time for Dr. Olena to fix that burn."

"I'm okay." Taylor smiled, then his knees buckled.

Julie grabbed him, and he swayed against her but stayed on his feet. He smelled like dirt after a rain. "No, you're not. Let's go."

"It's just the adrenaline wearing off," Taylor offered weakly.

They limped to the doors. The crowd had disappeared, and they were alone in the entrance hall. "I think we should play hooky for the rest of the day," Julie suggested.

Taylor managed a chuckle. "Dr. Olena will fix this burn in two seconds. I doubt I'll get any sick days out of Kaplan."

"There are only a few hours of afternoon left, and we've achieved enough for one day." Julie grinned. "I know this cool little place with all-you-can-eat dim sum."

They stepped out into the sunshine and headed for the ER. Taylor gave her a weary smile. "That sounds good to me."

It was dark by the time Julie drove down the familiar narrow street in Bay Ridge and saw her home, the lights in the bottom story looking golden and cozy on the dingy street. It felt like a century since she had last been here.

She stepped out of Genevieve as she hit the button to open the garage door, in case her landlady had forgotten to close the back door again and her little dog ended up in the street. It was soundly closed. Breathing a sigh of relief, Julie pulled the car into the garage.

As she got out, the back door opened. Blue TV light haloed the little figure of Julie's landlady, Lillie, whose white hair was neatly combed and up in a bun tonight. "Julie, dear! I'm so glad you're home. I was worried."

Julie checked her phone for the time. Half past seven. The hours had flown in that dim sum place with the newly healed Taylor. "Sorry, Lillie. I should have called."

"Not at all, dear." Lillie beamed. "How's your head?"

Julie touched the tender spot on the back of her skull. It was nothing compared to the nasty bruise and abrasion on her elbow or the black-and-blue pattern over her ribs. Dr. Olena, the Sylthana Elf who ran the Para-ER, had given her more Tylenol and told her to soak in a hot bath. "Oh, it's fine." She smiled, tugging her sleeve down to hide her elbow. "Hey, I was going to cook a big pot of stew for us. We could freeze some to last for the next few days."

"Sounds good, dear. Should I make some rice?" Lillie asked.

"It's okay, Lillie. Thanks." Julie grabbed Hat from the dashboard and crumpled him under her arm as she closed the door. "Hey, how about we go for that road trip this weekend? I don't have anything on."

Lillie cackled. "That sounds good. It's about time you felt what Genevieve can do on the open road."

"I won't be home tomorrow night, though." Julie hesitated. "I'm going to a wedding."

"A wedding?" Lillie's eyes gleamed behind her thick glasses. "Are you taking that hottie from work with you?"

"Lillie!" Julie's cheeks burned.

"My, that is a *fine* specimen of a man." Lillie leered. "Wear something classy, honey. A girl like you doesn't have to do a thing to get the attention of a man like him, but judging from the way he hung around here last week when you were hurt, you've already got it."

Julie groaned. "Okay, Lillie. I'll be down with the stew a bit later."

"Looking forward to it, dear." Lillie backed away, muttering to her dog and cat, and closed the door.

Funny old bat, Hat commented as Julie mounted the creaky steps to her apartment. *Imagine you and Taylor together.*

Julie did not allow herself to do so. *Ha. Imagine.*

She flicked on the lights and sighed. "Clearly, cleaning wasn't on my to-do list this weekend."

"Cut yourself a little slack." Hat wriggled out from under her arm and bounced onto the kitchen counter. "You were concussed."

"I guess." Julie started the coffee machine and opened the fridge to get out the veggies for the stew. She started peeling potatoes.

She'd finished the potatoes and started on the carrots when Hat stirred on the counter. "Hey, Julie?"

"Uh-huh?" Julie tossed some peels into the trash.

"Back in the cavern, the way you got everyone to work together. I was..." He stopped.

"Impressed?" Julie smirked. "It's okay. You can say the word. Just two syllables. *Im-pressed.*"

"Now I'm not saying it," Hat muttered.

Julie grinned at him and started on the stew. Once it was bubbling on the stove, she flopped down at the kitchen table and tugged out her phone. There was a text from Taylor, a single goat emoji.

"This dude and the goat," she grumbled, scrolling through her chats. A name caught her eye: *Mom*. "Ugh. I should probably call my mom and let her know I'm still alive."

"Why?" Hat snorted. "It's not like she knows you spent today fighting off an army of Yetis and an insane troll."

"All the better. She's freaking out enough, just thinking it's my first day back at work after my concussion." Julie dialed her mother's number and held the phone a few inches away from her ear.

Her mom's shriek was still piercing. *"Juliaaaaaaaa!"*

"Hey, Mom." Julie turned down the stew, which was simmering.

"How's your head, darling? Did you take those turmeric pills I left you? It's not enough to just eat curry, you know. You need a larger dose to deal with the inflammation," Mom babbled.

"My head's fine, thanks. I had a good day at work, and now I'm home, cooking."

"Oh, good!" Mom chirped. "Those turmeric pills work great, don't they? So much more natural and with lots fewer side effects than that nasty chemical stuff the doctor gives you."

"Pretty sure they don't have side effects because they don't have *effects*, Mom."

"Don't be silly, honey. Natural is always better! Now that you've seen how well the turmeric pills work, you'll try the aloe vera juice, won't you? I'll send you another box."

"No!" Julie blurted. "I mean, no, thank you, Mom. I still have enough for a while."

"Good. Is it keeping you regular? Constipation can be very distracting at work, you know."

Julie closed her eyes and leaned back in her chair. "Everything's fine in that department." It was best to let Hurricane Aloe Vera Juice blow over her instead of trying to resist it.

"Wonderful!" Mom gave a coarse chuckle. "Although I have to say, if I was working with that nice young Taylor, constipation would be the *least* of my distractions."

Julie pondered the sink, wondering if she should throw her phone into it and drown it with the dishes. "Sure, Mom. Hey, I've got to go. I was just checking in. Is everything okay there?"

"Of course, baby. Everything's fine. Ernesto sends his love," Mom added.

Julie doubted it. There was nothing wrong with the man her mother had married, but whatever was between them, it wasn't love. "Okay. Love you."

"Love you."

Julie hung up and stifled a yawn. She was about to lock her phone and put it away when her eye caught a bunch of notifications from her banking app.

"That's weird," she mumbled. "I didn't use my card today except for the dim sum place."

"I'm still amazed you won't let Taylor pay for you. He *does* have a trust fund," Hat pointed out.

Julie tapped the app. "That's not the point. I can pay my own way, even if I don't… *Shit the bed!*"

"I should hope not."

"No, not that." Julie flapped a hand at him as she stared at her bank balance. It couldn't be right. She felt cold all over and tapped on it. There must be a huge mistake. Was Qbiit's ally setting her up as a thief for some reason?

"Julie? What's wrong?" Hat prompted.

Julie scrolled down the list of transactions, heart pounding in her chest. She looked up slowly. "I-I have, like, a *lot* more money than I ever thought I would."

Hat paused. "Is that a bad thing?"

"It's not bad. Just a shock!" Julie laughed in disbelief. "You know that five thousand dollar bonus Kaplan promised us if we signed on a new recruit within two weeks?"

"That thing he said before you recruited the six Weres? Yeah, I remember." Hat's brim curled smugly.

"Well, he paid me that bonus for *every one of the Weres*," Julie muttered. "And another this afternoon with the reference 'Qbiit.' I didn't know we got bonuses for capturing deranged, murderous trolls."

Hat chuckled. "I'm fairly sure there's nothing about that in the file."

"There's something else, too." Julie swallowed. "The biggest deposit of all. Like, a few months' worth of my salary."

"Oh? Who's it from?"

"Julius Nox. There's a note with it." Tears stung her eyes as she read, "*You went above and beyond to save my son.*"

"Aw. Who knew Julius had a sweet side?" Hat quipped.

Julie scoffed. "Cut it out, Hat. We both know Julius is a softie." She thought about the way he'd looked at Qbiit. "Well, in *some* ways." She lowered her phone to her lap and leaned back in her chair. "What am I supposed to do with all this?"

"Nothing right now." Hat hopped onto the kitchen table and rubbed against her hand like a cat. "We'll do a crash course in financial management later. For now, just bask in it."

"Bask!" Julie shook out the adrenaline burning her hands and feet. "Dude, it's the most I can do to *breathe* through it." She laughed. "It's been kind of a hectic few weeks."

"Just kind of?" Hat laughed. "Let's recap. In the past few weeks, you learned that a paranormal world exists, feared for your life on numerous occasions, made friends with the king of vampires, became the PMA's top recruiter, helped a centaur protect his ranch, fought off a bunch of Yetis on three different occasions, and saved the vampire prince's life. I'm not sure what a *really* hectic week would look like."

"Eh." Julie shrugged. "I'll let you know when I have one."

"Please don't. It doesn't sound like anything I want to be involved in." Hat chuckled. "Don't you miss the peace and quiet of unemployment sometimes?"

Julie raised an eyebrow. "You mean the loneliness and imminent starvation?"

"You had plenty of time to read," Hat pointed out.

"Yeah, well, Mom was sort of right. There is more to the world than reading, but don't tell her I said that." Julie smiled. "Yeti fights or no Yeti fights, things are better now than they've been in a long time. I feel like…well, like I belong."

"As a recruiter?" Hat asked. "Don't you sometimes dream of bigger things?"

"I'm pretty happy with what I have right now," Julie admitted.

She grabbed her Chromebook from the table and flipped it open, then clicked on her email account. There was a bunch of spam and junk mail, but near the top, she saw a message marked HQ.

To All Agency Employees.

Your presence is requested at a memorial service for the fallen at 11:30 on Wednesday in the auditorium.

Your Captain

"Flowery writing," Julie commented.

Hat laughed. "He has to keep things streamlined in case human eyes see his emails."

"Uh-huh." Julie yawned widely and got up to check on the stew. "I can finish the cleaning tomorrow."

"Nap while the stew cooks," Hat suggested. "I'll keep an eye on it."

"Nah, I'm too wired for that. Suddenly having a bunch of money will do that to you." Julie's eyes strayed to the thick half-finished book on her nightstand. "Actually, I know just the way to pass the evening after a life-changing day."

Hat chuckled. Julie curled up in the comfortable chair beside her bed, picked up the book, and plunged into a different world. This one didn't contain any Yetis trying to kill her.

CHAPTER TEN

Julie let out a breath and smoothed the front of her gown as she looked into the mirror. Her heart fluttered in her chest. This dress had looked incredible at Iris Fashions in Avalon Village, but standing in her little apartment, it looked like something from another world.

It is something from another world, Hat pointed out.

Oh, shut up. Julie couldn't stop grinning. She turned this way and that, watching as the ballgown's poofy skirt shifted and shimmered in the cold electric light. The bodice was decorated with deep red roses and vines that twined over her chest, and the whole thing was as light as air.

"Oh, darling," Lillie murmured. "You look *incredible.*"

Julie turned. "Lillie! You didn't have to climb all those stairs."

"I thought I'd come up and give you a hand, dear. Tightening your corset and all that." Lillie shuffled across the floor, her wrinkled old face creasing in a bright grin, and ran a hand over the skirt. "My, my! What fabric *is* this?"

"I don't know," Julie confessed.

"Me neither. Never liked sewing. Driving's more my speed if you get my drift." Lillie cackled. "Do you need any help?"

Considering the dress had magically altered itself to fit like a second skin, Julie didn't, but she glanced at the diamond necklace on her nightstand.

Don't! Hat sputtered.

"Could you help me with my necklace?" Julie asked, resting a hand on the space between her collarbones.

"Ooh, look at that bling!" Lillie cooed. She scooped Hat, who was currently in the form of a beautiful diamond necklace, into her hands.

You'll regret this, Hat grumbled.

Julie smirked. "Isn't it lovely? I, uh, borrowed it from Taylor's sister." Her toes curled at the lie, but she couldn't expose sweet little Lillie to the paranormal world.

She turned to face the mirror, and Lillie gently looped the necklace around her neck and clasped it at the back. It sparkled on Julie's chest. Lillie's grin widened, and she squeezed the tops of Julie's arms. "You're beautiful, dear. Inside and out. Never, ever forget it."

"Aw, Lillie." Julie laid a hand over the older woman's. "Thank you."

A powerful engine purred outside, and Lillie raised her head. "I would know that sound anywhere! Is that a *Rolls?*"

Julie hurried to the window and groaned at the sight of the elegant silver vehicle waiting at the curb. She wondered if a Rolls Royce had ever been seen in this part of Brooklyn before. A white-gloved chauffeur opened the door, and Taylor stepped out in a smartly cut dusky-purple suit.

"Be still, my heart!" Lillie uttered dramatically.

Julie giggled. "Lillie!"

"He's quite something, but make no mistake, dear. So are you." Lillie smirked. "Go knock that young man's socks off, you understand?" She gave Julie a light slap on the ass. "Maybe more than his socks!"

Julie was still blushing as she made her way down the stairs,

Lillie helping with the back of her dress, and into the garage. Taylor had seen her in the dress since he'd bought it for her, but his eyes still popped.

"Hello," he managed huskily. "You look lovely."

Why, thank you, Hat murmured in a sultry voice.

Hat! Julie squealed. She smiled. "Done ogling? Can we go now?"

Lillie cackled.

"I wasn't—" Taylor's eyes widened, and he stared at Lillie. "Ms. Griswall, I promise I wasn't ogling or—"

"Relax, young man." Lillie pinched his cheek. "Show this young lady a good time, or you'll have me to reckon with."

Taylor nodded with the respect of a man who had stared down the double barrels of Lillie's shotgun. "Yes, ma'am."

The Rolls had a champagne fridge in the backseat. Taylor offered Julie some, but she shook her head. "Champagne on an empty stomach?"

"Oh, you came hungry?" Taylor raised an eyebrow.

"I'm assuming there's dinner," Julie told him. "I'm also assuming I'm *not* dinner."

"Of course there will be dinner." Taylor chuckled. "And Julius would sooner eat the Eternity Queen than you at this point."

Julie smirked. "Where are the Mitsubishi and the Audi? In the laundry?"

"What?" Taylor snorted. "Why would you say that?"

"Because you change cars like I change clothes." Julie toyed with the unfamiliar weight of the diamonds on her chest.

Cut it out! You're tickling me, Hat grouched.

Sorry.

"Call it a perk of being royalty." Taylor shrugged. "I like cars."

The Rolls purred through the gates of the Nox mansion and

halted in the courtyard, and Julie gasped. A creeper that hadn't been there yesterday spilled over one of the high white walls, improbably sprouting deep red roses that spelled out *Malcolm and Cassidy*. When the chauffeur held the door for her, an unbelievable scent filled the air, heady and thick and sweet and exotic as though roses, lavender, jasmine, honeysuckle, pine, and alyssum had been blended to create an incredible perfume.

"Julius has been busy in that greenhouse of his," Julie commented. She took Taylor's arm to get out of the Rolls, and her poofy dress rustled in protest as it was squeezed through the door.

"It's pretty cool," Taylor conceded.

A path lined with will o' the wisps in decorative glass jars led the way through Julius' rose garden and up to the front doors. Julie stared at the tiny creatures as they buzzed and hummed, glowing softly in their jars.

"Imported from Scotland," Taylor told her. "They're hard to get hold of. Finicky, too. Die for no reason if you get the humidity wrong. They also have a regrettable tendency to lead people into bogs to their doom."

"Macabre." Julie hesitated at the front doors. "There's going to be a ton of royalty in there, right?"

"Yes, but you've got nothing to worry about. You're the guest of honor." Taylor smirked. "I'm royalty, and I'm not so bad."

"Eh." Julie shrugged.

Taylor laughed. "Hey!"

They headed down a shining marble hall lined with more roses and will o' the wisps and then stepped into a vast ballroom that seemed to have been transplanted out of *Cinderella* instead of being a vampire's lair. Roses dripped from every surface; there were no pots or floral foam. It seemed as though they grew there naturally. In the air above, a huge glass ball contained hundreds of will o' the wisps that drifted quietly around, their silver glow filling the room. Two rows of white satin couches lined the dance floor, with an aisle down the middle scattered with rose petals and glowing golden things the size of Julie's thumb. The couches faced a raised area up two steps, where an archway of roses waited.

Julie kept staring as Taylor led her down the aisle. "What *are* these, anyway?"

"Scrambled golden goose eggs," Taylor informed her.

Julie stopped dead, the golden stuff crunching under her feet. "Wait, this is *real* gold?"

Taylor's lip twitched. "Come on. Our seats are in the front since you're a guest of honor."

Soft music emanated from a huge scarlet bird—a greater Egyptian firebird, her training told her—sitting on a gold perch on one side of the room. Julie sank onto one of the super-comfy couches and gave the elf beside her a nervous smile. "Hey."

The elf grinned back, and Julie noticed that the corners of her eyes crinkled as she smiled. "Good evening."

"Oh, hey, Ilsa." Taylor flopped down beside Julie. "I guess it's no surprise you were invited."

"I'm startled to see you here." Ilsa arched an elegant eyebrow. "You're usually not one for these kinds of things."

"Oh, I wasn't invited. I'm a plus-one." Taylor gestured at Julie. "Ilsa, this is my partner at the PMA, Julie. This is my older sister Ilsanthia. You know, the crown princess."

"Hey, Your Highness," Julie spluttered.

Ilsa gave a chiming laugh. "No need for that. You must be the human who keeps getting my brother into trouble."

"Uh..." Julie bit her lip.

Ilsa's grin widened. "He needed a little more trouble in his life."

The music reached a crescendo, and silence fell among the guests. Julie leaned over and whispered in Taylor's ear. "She's a lot cooler than Shae."

"Some blobs of lava are a lot cooler than Shae," Taylor mumbled.

Julius was underneath the arch. He held up his hands, and the music abruptly ceased. "Friends." He beamed. The haggard look was gone from his eyes, which shone. "It's my honor to have you all here to celebrate the handfasting of my beloved son. I'll save the real speech for the dinner, but allow me to welcome you to my home and into the lives of these two young people." He bowed slightly. "I give you my son, Malcolm Nox!"

There was a smattering of applause. Julie joined in after a moment's hesitation. She glanced at Taylor, who gave her an encouraging smile.

Malcolm strode to the arch, grinning, his fangs shining in the light of the will o' the wisps. Julie had never seen him in a suit, but tonight he wore midnight blue with a silver tie that glowed with its own light. He looked ten years older and happy enough that sheer willpower seemed to be the only thing keeping his feet on the floor.

"Salamander skin," Taylor whispered to her. "Pricey."

The music started again, the firebird's chest swelling as he sang, and a gasp ran through the guests. Julie craned her neck to see Cassidy coming down the aisle. Her bridal gown was composed of foaming water—*real* water, rushing and hissing like the sea, and it cradled her figure and spilled down in a long skirt that ended in a train that broke like a wave. The smell of the sea filled the air as Cassidy passed them. She was beaming from ear to ear, and her eyes were fixed on Malcolm.

"Whoa," Julie murmured.

Taylor smirked. "I told you Iris is the best."

Malcolm stared at Cassidy, slack-jawed, visibly trembling as she came toward him. Her smile turned shy, and he mumbled something Julie couldn't hear as they grasped one another's hands, crossing their wrists.

Julius stepped forward, holding a white ribbon. He gave

Malcolm an encouraging smile, and after clearing his throat a couple of times, the young vampire managed to find his voice.

"I, Cassidy…" he croaked.

There was silence.

Cassidy's smile widened. "No, that's *my* name."

Laughter rippled through the crowd. Malcolm chuckled. "I, Malcolm Nox, take you, Cassidy Consta, to be my wedded wife 'til death us do part, and thereto I pledge my troth."

Julius wrapped one end of the ribbon around Malcolm's wrists and nodded at Cassidy. Her pure, high voice rang through the room as she echoed Malcolm's words. Julius wrapped the other end of the ribbon around her wrists, then laid his hands over theirs, smiling so hard that it seemed like the top of his head was about to come off.

In unison, the young vampires recited the next part of their vows. "You are flesh of my flesh, bone of my bone, blood of my blood. We are one and will be one until the last moon rises."

Julius' eyes shimmered with tears. He raised his hands, holding up Malcolm and Cassidy's, still intertwined. "I give you Malcolm and Cassidy Nox!" he thundered.

The guests cheered. This time, it was easy for Julie to join in.

The white couches vanished by magic, as did the aisle and the arch. Julie and Taylor were sitting at one of the long banquet tables on the raised area where the arch had been. Julius beamed over a glass of what Julie hoped was red wine at the head of the table while Julie and Taylor faced Malcolm and Cassidy. Kaplan sat on Taylor's left, chatting with Julius. He was wearing a tobacco-brown suit.

The sleeve of Cassidy's whitewater gown brushed the red tablecloth as she reached for her goblet but didn't wet it. She grinned at Julie. Malcolm's arm was wrapped around her shoulders.

"To you, little human." She raised the goblet.

Julie felt her cheeks burn, but she held up her goblet, too. "To me, I guess?"

Taylor chuckled, and glasses clinked around them. Julie sipped from her goblet, which contained an excellent nutty liqueur. Waiters appeared, all as silent as Perkins, and gold plates were set in front of each guest. Julie looked down with interest as the waiter lifted a gold cover off her dessert. It was a slice of death by chocolate cake.

"Ooh, yes." Julie picked up her fork, which was also gold. "My favorite."

Cassidy laughed. "Of course it is."

Julie stared at her. "Uh, explain?"

"These are cornucopia plates." Taylor tapped his, which contained a perfect souffle. "Whatever your favorite dish is, that's what appears when the lid is lifted."

"Okay, then." Julie took a bite and groaned with pleasure. "That explains why I had butter prawns for a starter and that really good ribeye for the entree."

Malcolm smiled at his chocolate lava cake, which bled molten chocolate everywhere. "I can't believe this is your first time eating from a cornucopia plate."

Julie grinned. "I hope it's not my last."

Somehow I doubt it. Hat snorted. *By the way, are you ever going to talk to Malcolm? I can feel your pitch buzzing around in your head, and it's making me itchy.*

Okay, let's see. Julie took another bite of cake to buy herself a little time before speaking. "Malcolm, I guess you and Cassidy are going to stay here with your dad?"

"Yes, well." Malcolm shrugged. "My suite is big enough for both of us."

"Although we're going to have to do something about the bachelor-pad vibe," Cassidy added.

Malcolm kissed her cheek. "It's not like I'm a bachelor anymore, is it?"

"Of course not, and you're not going to be playing video games all day, either." Cassidy arched an eyebrow.

Malcolm sighed. "What else am I supposed to do?" He lowered his voice. "Our sire still won't involve me in running things."

"I have an idea about that." Julie leaned forward. "How would you feel about joining the PMA?"

"Julie!" Taylor hissed. "Here? Seriously?"

Julie waved him away. "Come on, Malcolm. You know you're destined for bigger things than video games. Working at the PMA could give you the experience you need to become the leader your dad and I both believe you will be someday."

Cassidy nudged him. "Listen to her. She's got good ideas."

"Cass!" Malcolm stared at her.

"You need something to give you purpose, love." Cassidy shrugged and turned back to her dessert. "This could be it."

"She's not wrong." Julie sipped her liqueur. "You'd be an asset to the PMA."

Malcolm took another bite of his lava cake. "It sounds less boring than playing games all day."

"Stop being an insufferable wimp, Malcolm," Kaplan snarled. He leaned over Taylor, who shrank back in his chair.

The vampire blinked. "Uncle Jack?"

"You need to do something with your life, and you know it, son." Kaplan wagged a huge finger at him. "Meadows is right. You would be good for the PMA and vice versa. Besides, I have a special job in mind for you."

"You do?" Julie blurted.

Kaplan glared at her.

"Sir?" she added.

"I do." Kaplan folded his massive arms. "I've been looking for a junior officer to train as my interdepartmental coordinator. I have to do far too much shouting at the recruiters."

Julie toyed with the idea of sticking out her tongue but thought better of it.

"You'd have to work your way up the ranks to qualify for the position," Kaplan added, "but it's a good one."

Malcolm stared down at his plate, then up at Kaplan, and his smile struggled to break free. "I'd be working with you, Uncle Jack?"

"You would." Kaplan nodded. "And you'd call me 'sir.'"

"I can do that, sir." Malcolm's smile exploded on his face. "Thank you. I'd love that."

"Good." Kaplan knocked back the last of his mahua, the nut liqueur. "Why is nobody dancing?"

The dance floor was empty, although its gleaming marble, lined with more of the will o' the wisp jars, was inviting.

"Someone needs to break the ice," Malcolm suggested.

"Aren't you doing a first dance?" Julie asked.

Cassidy stared at her. "A first what?"

"Never mind." Julie raised both hands. "Clearly a human thing."

"Someone needs to get this party started." Kaplan pushed back his chair, buttoned his coat, and strode toward the dance floor.

Julie stared at Taylor. "What is happening?"

"I have no idea," Taylor admitted.

The firebird was still on his perch, singing his heart out. Kaplan strode onto the dance floor and gave the bird a sharp glance. Abruptly, the soft, melodic tune changed to a brisk tune with a beat.

Every eye was on the floor, occupied at that moment only by an enormous weretiger. Kaplan's amber eyes burned, and he dropped down to a full split.

"What the *f—*" Julie began.

A cheer rose from everyone at the tables, drowning out her words. Kaplan jumped to his feet in perfect time with the music and began street dancing, his huge limbs moving as though mechanized, feet as quick as a deer's and absolutely silent on the floor.

Julie couldn't stop laughing. Taylor's mouth was hanging open.

The next thing she knew, Kaplan was breakdancing, spinning and twirling, legs up, head down, then flipping to his feet and turning a double backflip that ended in a freeze on one leg as he glared defiantly at the audience.

The cheer rocked the mansion.

Taylor jumped to his feet, grabbing Julie's hand. "Consider this party started!"

She was still laughing as he towed her to the dance floor.

CHAPTER ELEVEN

Taylor had swapped out last night's purple suit for his green dress uniform with shining silver buttons. He was standing outside the auditorium, shifting uncomfortably from foot to foot, when Julie stepped out of the elevator. The muted rumble of voices filled the air, coming from the open doors of the auditorium.

"I hate funerals," Julie mumbled as she approached Taylor.

"It's not a funeral," Taylor told her.

Julie winced. "Not so loud."

"No?" Taylor raised both eyebrows. "The liqueur *was* good, wasn't it?"

"Uh-huh." Julie grimaced. "Did Kaplan really do a backflip, or was I drunk by then?"

"You only got drunk near the end." Taylor laughed. "When that woodland sprite gave you Bacchus wine, and you didn't pay attention when I tried to stop you."

"Oh, yeah." Julie flinched. "That." She stifled a yawn. "Wait, you said that this isn't a funeral?"

"It's not. It's a memorial ceremony to honor the fallen in front of the whole PMA and also to honor their families."

Julie's stomach clenched at the word. She briefly remembered sitting in the church where Dad's funeral was held, listening to the quiet sobbing around her and wanting nothing more in the world than to run into his arms. She sucked in a breath. "Let's get this over with."

Taylor's grim mask slipped back into place. "You ready?"

She nodded. "More ready than ever."

They headed into the auditorium, and this time, all the seats were crammed. They squeezed into a spot near the back. The stage's curtains were a velvety black, and images of the six fallen shone on the big screen. Julie's eyes dwelled on Leafeyes and Palladius. The pictures at the briefing had come from their ID badges, but these photos looked like they'd been pulled from social media. In his photo, Palladius was beaming as he held up a shining rainbow trout. He had a wooden pipe wedged into the corner of his mouth. Leafeyes' pretty young wife had her arms around him, and three little elves spilled over his knees and shoulders as he sat in a leather armchair, wearing a heinously ugly Christmas sweater.

Julie's throat tightened.

I'm sorry, Hat murmured. He was a green service cap today, matching her dress uniform. *You asked, but I didn't want to tell you.*

It's okay. Julie clenched her hands in her lap. *They were good to me, Hat. They never mentioned that I was human, even though everyone else did. It's not right that they died.*

The auditorium doors opened again, and on silent feet, Kaplan paced up to the stage. His face was gray and set, deeply lined, and Julie was sure last night's wine had nothing to do with it. He stood still for a moment, staring at the pictures of the people Qbiit had killed. Julie saw his big hands curl into fists and knew exactly how he felt.

Kaplan turned to the assembled crowd, and silence fell. The weretiger's chest heaved, then he spoke.

"This afternoon, the troll responsible for the deaths of these fine paranormals will stand trial." Kaplan squared his shoulders. "However, no amount of justice can bring them back. These individuals died trying to stop mind-controlled Yetis from destroying the Para-Military Agency. We do not yet know what the Yetis wanted in HQ or where they were heading, but we can be certain that if they had broken through into the main building, the consequences would have been disastrous. That was averted by the selfless and courageous actions of these six individuals, and we honor them for being some of the best among us."

Last night's firebird swooped into the room, his wings almost soundless, and perched on the lectern beside Kaplan. He nodded, and the bird raised his gold beak and began to sing a very different tune from the one Julie had heard him sing during Malcolm's handfasting last night.

The firebird's voice rang out in a simple, haunting song, each note slow and drawn out, poignant and piercing. It made tears sting Julie's eyes, and she fought to hold them back as everyone in the auditorium rose to their feet and stood to attention. Julie's white-gloved hands trembled by her sides.

Measured footsteps punctuated the firebird's song. Two rows of officers marched into the room, resplendent in red dress uniforms. The elves, dwarves, orcs, and hard-bitten Weres moved slowly toward the stage. Taking positions on either side of the aisle between seats, they stood to attention, forming an honor guard.

There was a rustle from the front seats, and six paranormals left their places and stepped up to the stage. Julie's heart clenched. One was a bent old dwarf, her hair silver with age, her head bowed, crying. The other was the beautiful elf from Leafeyes' photo. She stood very straight, but she was trembling uncontrollably, and she wrung a handkerchief in her hands, squeezing and folding.

A silvery glow filled the room. Six Starlight Fae girls, the light emanating from their hair and skin between white and silver, walked up to the stage as the honor guard saluted. They each carried a folded flag of the Eternity Throne and wore long black gowns that glittered with starlight at the hems.

The firebird's song reached a crescendo as the fae arrived on the stage. One by one, they gave the folded flags to the next of kin of the fallen. The dwarf—Palladius' mother, Julie guessed—was sobbing so hard that she could barely reach out and take the flag. Leafeyes' wife's face was still, but when the fae laid the flag in her hands, her knees sagged as though she would collapse under its weight.

The firebird was still as the Starlight Fae left the room. The next of kin turned to face Kaplan, who took several deep breaths before speaking.

"Your loved ones died valiantly." His voice rumbled through the room. "They saved countless lives by sacrificing their own. They will never be forgotten, and we will seek justice for what happened to them."

Kaplan looked up, his eyes sweeping the auditorium, and he pointed at the pictures on the screen. "They died protecting you," he rumbled. "They died performing the mission that is the objective of the PMA as a whole: defending the Eternity Throne, upholding the good, protecting the innocent, and preserving peace in the paranormal world. Are you willing to go to that extent to protect our world? Are you willing to give yourselves as these people did?"

Julie's breath caught in her chest. She barely knew what Kaplan meant, but she was aware that everyone in this room was rapt and silent. His words had touched them all.

"The PMA has a sacred duty to protect us paranormals. May we be as deeply bound to that duty as these people were, and may we find and stop the one responsible for these killings." Kaplan's voice rose. "May we give ourselves to our duty as thoroughly as they did."

A sacred duty to the Eternity Throne. Julie had parroted those words to new recruits, but looking at Leafeyes' smile and Palladius' friendly grin on the screen, she thought she understood them for the first time.

"Thunderbirds, stand by!" Kaplan called.

Wind rushed through the auditorium, tearing at Julie's clothes and making Hat pin himself to her head in panic. Three enormous birds swooped in and hovered above the stage, their wings barely fluttering. They were the size of eagles but as black as crows, and their eyes, feet, and beaks were silver like lightning.

Kaplan turned to face them. As one, everyone in the auditorium raised their hands to their foreheads in salute. Julie was a beat slower than everyone else.

"Ready!" Kaplan barked.

The thunderbirds hovered, wings outstretched.

"Now!" Kaplan roared.

BOOM!

The birds clapped their wings and thunder ripped through the air, shaking the ground under Julie's feet.

"Ready! Now!"

BOOM!

"Ready! Now!"

BOOM!

Julie held it together as the firebird began to sing again. It sounded like *Taps*, but it was older and fiercer and more pure. It was only when Leafeyes' wife returned to her seat, and the three little elves threw their arms around her and sobbed and her composure shattered so that she bent double and gave a terrible, keening wail that Julie could no longer hold back her tears.

Julie pushed back her chair. "I'm going to lunch."

Their office had been oppressively quiet since the memorial.

Taylor looked up from a pile of paperwork, his eyes vague. "Okay."

"I'm going to grab it on the go and eat with Qtana in the ER. I promised her I would, and then all this happened." Julie shrugged. "Do you want to come?"

The elf shook his head. "I'm not hungry. I'm going to finish up here."

"Okay." Julie grabbed Hat, now back to being a cute beige Panama, then hesitated. "Hey, Taylor?"

"Uh-huh?"

"Are you okay?"

He looked up, and a faint smile flickered over his face. "Yeah. Just hungover. And the memorial service..." He sucked in a breath. "It was rough."

"We'll figure out who Qbiit was working for." Julie rammed Hat onto her head. "And we'll make sure he never hurts anyone again."

"Singlehandedly, huh?" Hat commented.

"Oh, shut up, Hat. I'm having a moment," Julie scolded.

That got a dry chuckle out of Taylor. Julie left him in the office and headed to the cafeteria, which was, as usual, filled with paranormals sitting at three long tables. She headed for the buffet table and grabbed a couple of excellent beef sandwiches to go, then headed for the elevator and the Para-ER.

When she strode into the ER, Dr. Olena was bent over the reception desk, signing papers. She looked up at the sound of Julie's footsteps and grinned. "Oh, hey, Julie! I don't have your blood results yet if you were looking for them."

"I wasn't looking for them." Julie held up the sandwiches. "I was smuggling food to one of your inmates. I hear you're holding Qtana hostage."

"Drama queen." Dr. Olena chuckled. "Poor troll. Her injuries were too severe to be healed entirely by magic, so she's in a private room until she gets better. Sounds like she's a heroine. Kaplan ordered only the best for her."

"I'm looking forward to hearing the whole story. Want to join us for lunch?" Julie gestured with a sandwich.

"Not right now, but thanks." Dr. Olena pointed into the medical unit. "Second hallway on your left. Room Six."

"Thanks." Julie followed the Sylthana Elf's pointing finger to the right room and knocked on the door with an elbow since her hands were occupied. "Qtana?" she called softly. "It's me. Are you awake?"

"Julie!" Qtana's voice was surprisingly strong. "Come in."

Julie pushed the door open and shuffled into the nicest hospital room she'd ever seen. Ignoring the hospital bed, drip stands, and monitors, it could have been a cute bedroom in a Manhattan apartment. There was artsy floral wallpaper, a big window overlooking the campus, and a dresser in one corner covered with flowers and cards. One of the flowers snapped its teeth at Julie as she passed it.

"My brother has a sick sense of humor," Qtana apologized.

The troll was sitting up in bed, her cheeks still the palest green, but she wore a faint smile. She absently scratched at the catheter in the back of her hand, then lowered it to the bed.

"I brought lunch." Julie held out one of the wrapped sandwiches.

"Ooh! Thank you." Qtana took it.

"Looking at your room, I'm guessing it wasn't necessary." Julie grinned and plopped into the armchair beside the bed. "They must be feeding you like a princess."

"Oh, no." Qtana grimaced. "Hospital food is hospital food everywhere, I think."

"Well, *bon appetit,* then." Julie unwrapped her sandwich.

Qtana took a bite of hers, then glanced sideways at Julie from under her glasses. "Um, I'm glad you came. I, uh, I haven't had the chance to thank you for...for what you guys did. Qbiit was going to kill me."

"Taylor's the one who saved you." Julie shrugged.

"Kaplan told me you were the leader of the expedition. I'm serious, Julie. I would have died if it wasn't for you." Pink spots appeared on Qtana's cheeks. "I don't know how I can repay you."

Kaplan's been bragging about you, Hat noted.

"Don't give me that repaying bullshit." Julie waved a hand. "I'm just glad you're okay. It was a scary moment, seeing Qbiit standing over you like that. What even happened?"

Qtana looked away. "You'd be less kind to me if you knew."

Julie frowned. "What do you mean?"

The troll picked at her sandwich, staring at nothing. "You think I'm the victim, but the truth is, I was a major part of the whole thing."

Shock rippled through Julie's veins, ice-cold. "What do you mean?" She kept her voice under control.

"It...well, it started a couple of months ago. Just before you joined the PMA." Qtana swallowed hard. "Qbiit approached me with a proposal for a new project that would blend science and magic and push the boundaries of both. It sounded exciting and like it would do some good in the world."

Julie leaned forward. *That is the Qtana I know.*

Hear her out, Hat encouraged.

"Qbiit was working on a project that would enable automatic telepathic translation between paranormal languages. It would have been groundbreaking, considering how broadly language differs among paranormal groups, particularly the far-flung ones." She glanced at Julie, her blush deepening. "Groups like the Yetis."

Julie sat back in her chair. "I see where this is going."

"It wasn't long after you joined that Kaplan pulled me off the IRSA team and reassigned me to magical communications full-time so I could focus on the project. I thought it would do good, Julie. I thought it was all aboveboard."

Qtana squeezed her eyes shut. "I made good progress. Technomagical telepathic translation would have changed so much. Enabled us to reach communities of paranormals that don't even know the Eternity Throne exists. It would be like opening a door for hundreds of uncontacted peoples. However, I kept running into the same problem. The program had the potential to control minds, not just translate their thoughts."

Julie nodded. "And you couldn't fix it because Qbiit was counting on that."

"I think Qbiit built it into the program. He's good. He couldn't build the whole thing himself—he needed me for that—but he was good enough to stop me from fixing my code. I thought it wasn't being tested yet. I thought it could only be used after I'd fixed that."

Qtana shook her head. "Qbiit was using it the whole time, and the more I improved it, the more Yetis he could mind-control."

"What happened on Monday?" Julie asked.

"Right after we talked at breakfast, when I got to work, Qbiit was acting really weird. He kept getting angrier about IA being involved." Qtana sighed. "In hindsight, he'd kidnapped Malcolm since vampire blood was one of the components that would strengthen the technomagical process, and he was getting nervous. I thought he was acting shady, so I checked in with our upper management to make sure everything was okay. They told me Qbiit hadn't reported any progress on our project in weeks, even though I made a major breakthrough just last week."

Qtana winced. "I expanded the range of our system so you could use it across the Veil, from here to Avalon or vice versa."

"I see." Julie bit her lip. "That's why things escalated so fast."

"Exactly." Qtana's shoulders sagged. "Something was wrong, so I confronted Qbiit."

"You confronted him?" Julie raised her eyebrows. "You go, girl. He's intimidating."

"I couldn't stand the thought that my system was being misused." Qtana gritted her teeth. "The confrontation didn't go well. One minute we were arguing, and the next, I said I was going to tell Kaplan. Qbiit grabbed a monitor and knocked me out with it."

"Ouch," Julie sympathized.

Qtana touched her bandaged head. "I'm lucky he didn't kill me. He only kept me alive because he couldn't run the system without my help. When I woke up in the Yeti cavern, he forced me to keep working on the system and expanding it. He wanted to control more Yetis at once."

Her eyes widened. "He was planning some kind of attack. He never told me what it would be on, but he was going to do something terrible." She sucked in a breath. "I'm glad you stopped him. I wish I had been strong enough to do it myself."

Julie put a hand on the troll's wrist, carefully avoiding the IV line. "You did well, all things considered."

A Sphynx sashayed out of the aether, appearing from nowhere, and sat on Qtana's nightstand. The cat devoted a few moments to knocking a pill bottle off the nightstand before turning his giant yellow eyes on Qtana. "Thank you for your testimony, troll. It will be useful at Qbiit's trial."

"What the… Where did… How…" Qtana sputtered.

"Where'd you come from?" Julie demanded. "Have you been listening all this time?"

The Sphynx yawned and curled his tail around his paws. "Someone had to make sure you were innocent, which you clearly are. Don't look so horrified. You have nothing to worry about."

"You've got to stop spying on people," Julie sassed.

"Calm yourself, little human," the Sphynx purred. He turned

back to Qtana. "Is there anything else you can tell me about your time with Qbiit that might be useful?"

Qtana bit the inside of her cheek. "I think so. When I was waking up in the cavern, I heard him talking to someone. At least, I heard him talking. He sounded like he was taking orders. I never heard another person. Maybe I hallucinated it, but this doesn't seem like the kind of thing Qbiit could come up with on his own."

"Very good. Thank you." The Sphynx rose, knocking a few cards off the nightstand, and turned to Julie. "Your presence is required at Qbiit's trial, young human. Taylor Woodskin's, too. Qtana is excused from testifying in person due to the state of her health, but you two have three hours to make your way to the courthouse in Avalon Village."

"The courthouse?" Julie's heart stuttered, and she squeezed her hands into fists. "I'll be there. Anything to nail that son of a bitch for what he did." She thought about Leafeyes' sobbing wife.

"My, my." The Sphynx chuckled. "My friend Cerberus would be appalled at your language, young lady."

"I've got worse in mind for Qbiit," Julie snarled. She got up. "Hope you feel better soon, Qtana. I'll stop by again tomorrow."

The troll smiled weakly. "Thanks."

Julie headed out and strode toward the door with brisk steps.

Easy, Hat chided, bouncing on her head. *The courthouse isn't going to evaporate, you know. It won't take you that long to get there.*

I just can't wait to see that sucker stand trial. Julie flexed her fingers. *I want to know who put him up to this. We've got to stop them, Hat.*

Although I find your one-woman crusade charming, you could walk slower, Hat grumbled.

"Julie!"

Julie stopped as Dr. Olena jogged up to her, clutching a clipboard, her brow furrowed. "What's up, Doc?"

Really? Hat sighed.

"Nothing, I think." Dr. Olena waved the clipboard. "I just got your blood results back, and there are a few..." she paused, "discrepancies."

"Discrepancies?" Julie raised her eyebrows. "Like what? I've never had trouble with my bloodwork before."

"I don't think it's anything to worry about." Dr. Olena glanced at the clipboard. "It's just that the gene that's supposed to be present in your DNA—the one that enabled you to see the paranormal world when you tasted our food at the fake drafting breakfast—is not here."

Julie frowned. "What?"

"My thoughts exactly." Dr. Olena grimaced. "There's only one conclusion. There must have been a mix-up of blood samples at the lab. It happens sometimes."

"Oh." Julie's shoulders relaxed. "So, you need to redo the tests?"

"Pretty much. Sorry about that. I already treated you like a pincushion the last time." Dr. Olena held up a fistful of tubes. "Do you have time to give me a few more samples?"

"Sorry, Dr. Olena. Not right now." Julie checked her watch. "I've got to get to the courthouse for Qbiit's trial."

"That's okay." Dr. Olena waved the clipboard. "It's not urgent. When you're free."

"Okay. Thanks." Julie smiled. "I'll see you after the trial."

"See you."

Julie was halfway to the doors when Dr. Olena called her name again. "Julie!"

She turned, and the Sylthana Elf's face had hardened into a collection of fierce lines. "Yeah?"

Dr. Olena squared her shoulders. "Make sure that son of a bitch goes away for a long, long time."

"That's the plan," Julie promised.

After she got out of the elevator near their office, Taylor almost bumped into her. He was staring down at his phone and jumped when she appeared. "Oh, there you are! Good timing. Kaplan just called. We've got to go to Avalon for the trial."

"I know." Julie led the way to their office and got her things together, then hooked her backpack over one shoulder. "One of the Sphynxes appeared to tell me."

Taylor raised an eyebrow. "A Sphynx decided he had to summon you to court in person when Kaplan could have just sent you a text?"

"He was listening in on Qtana's testimony." Julie grinned. "If what she said was true, Qbiit's not going to see the light of day for a while. Well, I don't know. The paranormal justice system might surprise me."

"I doubt it. It's not that different from yours." Taylor grabbed his keys.

Julie jingled Genevieve's. "Uh-uh. I don't think so. We're going in Genevieve this time."

"Come on, girl." Taylor sighed. "You're the one who keeps encouraging me to be more independent. Besides, I brought the Ferrari."

"No Ferrari can beat my Genevieve!" Julie cried dramatically and crashed out of the office.

Taylor followed her, grumbling, but they both knew it was no use arguing.

CHAPTER TWELVE

Leaving Genevieve in a parking garage, Julie and Taylor stepped under the 110th Street Bridge at the edge of Central Park. There was the familiar lurch of stepping through a portal, and when Julie's swimming vision cleared, they were in Avalon Village.

Even though she'd been here before, Julie's stomach still flipped with excitement at the sight of the bustling plaza filled with paranormals. It was sunny in Avalon today, and the light sparkled on the many-colored cobblestones and the brightly colored flags and banners that were everywhere. The shops lining the plaza were as busy as ever. As Taylor hurried along the sidewalk, Julie couldn't resist stopping in front of a smithy where a dwarf was turning a whetstone to sharpen a blade that buzzed and spat like electricity.

"A lightning blade. Powerful but unpredictable," Taylor told her. "Come on. We're going to be late."

"How far is the courthouse?" Julie asked, reluctantly peeling herself away from the smithy.

"Another twenty minutes' walk down First Street." Taylor checked his watch. "We're in good time."

"I've never testified before," Julie admitted.

"Me neither." Taylor grimaced. "Sorry. I know that wasn't very helpful. But Kaplan will be there. I'm sure he'll tell you what to do."

They stopped at the crossing to allow a carriage drawn by six pitch-black winged horses with flames streaming from their eyes and nostrils to rattle past, madly cackling, then crossed the street to turn left. Here, the buildings were far more uniform than the fairy-puke vibes of the plaza and Second Street. Stone buildings towered on either side, with banners and battlements and arrow slits.

"What's with all the wannabe castles?" Julie asked.

Taylor laughed. "These are official buildings. That's the Avalon Village branch of the PMA. It's more like a small police precinct since HQ is easily accessible by portal. This is the licensing department."

"Licensing department?" Julie stared at the squat building, which had cannons on the roof.

"What, did you think you could drive a carriage or ride a pegasus without one?" Taylor chuckled. "It took me three tries to pass my broomstick license."

"You can fly a broomstick?" Julie raised her eyebrows. "Ever played Quidditch?"

"Do I look like a nerd to you?" Taylor shot back. "It was on a dare. I was in trouble for *weeks* afterward."

The distant *thump* of giant wings caught Julie's attention. She looked up, her heart thudding at the memory of the last time she'd been here when a dragon had swooped so low over her that she'd smelled its smoky breath. This time, the dragon was in the distance, circling on a thermal over a huge building just visible over the rooftops. It was set on a hill, and it reached toward the sun, towers competing for height against the horizon. It shimmered.

"Whoa," Julie breathed.

Taylor followed her gaze. "The Eternal Palace."

"Cool."

They turned a corner, and a cacophony of voices filled the street, which was crowded from edge to edge with all kinds of supernaturals. A row of PMA agents in blue uniforms stood in front of the building at the end of the street that had stern granite battlements at the top and the Eternity Throne flag flying over the entry.

The crowd was barely moving, and Julie saw a lot of craned necks as people tried to see into the courthouse. She felt a tension in the air that made goosebumps rise on her arms.

"Why are there so many people here?" she asked.

"This is one of the highest-profile cases they've seen in years. I don't ever remember the PMA being breached before," Taylor told her.

Julie stayed close as Taylor shoved through the crowd. When they reached the agents in front of the building, the nearest one, an orc, held out a hand. "No entry," he growled.

"Taylor Woodskin and Julie Meadows." Taylor flashed his ID, and Julie did the same. "We're here to testify."

The agent nodded and let them through, and they strode under an iron portcullis and into a stone courtyard. When they stepped through the doors at the other side of the courtyard, Julie felt as though she'd been teleported into a courthouse in New York City. The reception area was quiet and carpeted, with wooden benches along the walls and a well-dressed Were receptionist typing on a computer.

"This way," Taylor murmured, leading Julie down a hall. "I was here with my parents once. The courtroom is down here."

Julie swallowed, heart thudding in her ears at the importance of what they were about to do. She wiped her palms on the uniform pants she'd put on at the PMA before leaving and took a calming breath.

Taylor led her to a guard standing outside the courtroom

doors, and they showed their IDs again. The doors swung open, and they marched into the courtroom.

Julie wasn't sure what she had been expecting, but it wasn't this circus.

The public gallery was crammed with paranormals of every description, standing room only. It overlooked the huge room. Julie saw elves and Weres and fae and a few creatures she couldn't begin to name. Men with goat feet, a lion with a goat head sprouting from its back, and a two-legged dragon that perched on the railing, flapping its reptilian wings and letting out a squawk from time to time.

Directly ahead was the judge's bench, and on Julie's left was a bench filled with paras juggling microphones and cameras and notebooks. Some were giving reports in English, and others in languages Julie didn't know. She heard a gargling Wookie noise and spotted a slender Yeti talking into one of the cameras, his voice low and tight.

"Here," Kaplan's familiar voice hissed. Julie spotted him sitting on the prosecution's side of the room, and she and Taylor made their way toward him. They slid onto the wooden bench beside him.

"The jury looks tense," Taylor whispered.

Julie glanced to her right, where the jury was sitting. There was a fae, a vampire, Aether and Sylthana Elves, an orc, a Were, and a Copper Dwarf.

Julie leaned closer to Taylor. "Is it just me, or is the jury comprised of the royal family groups?"

Taylor shrugged. "They're the most numerous groups."

There was a murmur through the gallery. Julie craned her neck back to see two burly orcs in blue uniforms marching down the aisle with Qbiit between them. An ugly black-and-purple bruise extended over the troll's face, his lip was split, and there was a bandage on his left arm. He wore iron shackles on his hands and feet, attached to a waist belt, and the chains jingled as he walked. His eyes found Julie's and narrowed as he passed. Julie considered blowing a raspberry but decided it was not the wisest move.

There was a yell from the gallery. A troll had stepped forward among the gathered paras, raising a fist. "Discrimination!" he shouted. "Justice for Qbiit!"

The Yeti who had been speaking to the media turned around with a cry, and a Were bailiff held up his hands to soothe him.

"Equality for non-magical paranormals!" the troll yelled. "Down with the royal families!"

A gasp rippled through the gallery. The Sylthana Elf group bridled. A bailiff walked toward the troll, who disappeared rapidly into the crowd.

A door in the back of the courtroom opened, and a tall fae strode into the room. She wore flowing black robes, and her long white hair hung down her back in complicated braids. When she took the bench, Julie felt as though she should curtsy. The fae had cool blue eyes that swept the courtroom, and Julie's stomach dropped. This woman oozed authority. She also looked like Judge Judy, and Julie thought about Lillie. She could hear the old lady's voice in her head. *That's a woman who knows her own mind!*

Silence fell before the fae took her seat, and an orc bailiff near the front stood. "All rise," he ordered.

Those in the room rose to their feet.

"The Eternal Court is now in session." The bailiff's voice tolled through the room like a bell. "Judge Penelope presiding—"

"We object!" The voice came from one of the Sylthana Elves, an imperious figure who strode to the front of the gallery. Roars of assent came from the elves gathered behind him. He swept his braids behind one pointed ear and glared at the judge. "This is a major case! Why is it being judged by a degenerate from a minority family that's dying out?"

Voices rose throughout the courtroom. The judge pressed her

lips together, and Julie turned to Taylor. "I don't get it. She's a fae."

"Not just any fae," Taylor muttered.

"The Lunar Fae dynasty is all but over!" one of the Sylthana Elves shouted, pushing through the crowd to stand beside the ringleader. "It's time for new leaders. New judges. A family that will represent the people!"

There was a roar of support from the defendant's side of the courtroom. The troll in the public gallery reappeared, waving a fist. "Justice for Qbiit!" he chanted. "Justice for Qbiit!"

"This trial should be presided over by a judge who represents the people!" the first Sylthana Elf yelled.

There was a bellow of assent from the gallery. The jury shifted in their seats. Kaplan let out a low, rumbling growl that made the floor quake beneath Julie's feet.

"Order!" the Lunar Fae judge called, tapping her gavel. "Order!"

The gallery was a mass of movement. Arms, wings, and claws waved. Paranormals got in each other's faces, yelling.

"What does it matter that she's a Lunar Fae?" a Were shouted from the gallery. "She's the best judge in Avalon! Let her try the case!"

"Justice for Qbiit!" the troll roared. Others had taken up his chant.

The Yeti had clasped his big hands to his ears and was shaking his head in fury. Julie couldn't blame him.

"Order!" the judge shouted. "Order!"

The bailiffs waded into the public gallery, prying apart paranormals who seemed to be on the brink of fighting. The troll was grabbed and restrained, and three bailiffs surrounded the Sylthana Elves.

"We have a right to be present at this trial!" the leader of the elves squealed, bunching his hands into fists.

"That is true, sir." The judge's eyes swept the gallery. "But this trial will be conducted in a civil and orderly manner, and anyone who does not settle down immediately will be summarily ejected from this courtroom."

Her words fell like slamming doors. The Sylthana Elf opened his mouth to protest, then fell silent.

"We may proceed." The judge sat down again, glancing at the bailiff. "Please continue, Officer Marino."

The orc cleared his throat. "Judge Penelope presiding," he went on. "Please be seated."

Julie sank onto the bench, whispering to Taylor, "Does it normally go like this?"

Taylor shrugged, but Kaplan had overheard. He leaned close. "No. The atmosphere here..." He growled. "Those Sylthana Elves are spoiling for a fight."

Julie glanced at Qbiit. The troll sat on the defendant's side across from Julie, and he flexed his wrists as though to test the restraints. He kept grinding his teeth. She could hear it from across the courtroom.

Judge Penelope ran an eye over the courtroom again, then nodded. "Good evening, ladies and gentlemen. Calling the case of the Eternity Throne versus Qbiit. Are both sides ready?"

A stern gray-haired man stood up from the attorney's table on the prosecution's side of the courtroom. "Ready for the Eternity Throne, Your Honor."

"Patrick Harrington," Kaplan murmured. "The Eternity Throne's DA. He's the best there is."

Next to Qbiit, another troll rose to his feet. "Ready for the defense, Your Honor."

The clerk of the court, a fae, swore in the jury at the judge's order. Harrington gave his opening statement, accusing Qbiit of crimes Julie knew he had committed, although she winced at the list of charges: muggings, the murders, and the kidnappings and attempted murders of Qtana and Malcolm. The mind-control of the Yetis was a charge all its own. There was an angry mutter from the gallery at this, but a glare from the judge silenced them.

The troll representing Qbiit stood up. "Your Honor, and ladies and gentlemen of the jury, under the law, my client is presumed innocent until proven guilty. This trial will reveal that my client was being manipulated, tricked, and mind-controlled by another." He shot a glance at Qbiit, who hung his head silently. "Therefore, my client is not guilty."

"Bullshit," Julie muttered.

"Shhh," Taylor hissed.

The judge nodded as Qbiit's lawyer sat down. "The prosecution may call its first witness."

Harrington nodded. "The Eternity Throne calls Horusirison-tubiskhenmonset from the internal affairs division of the Official Para-Military Agency."

The Sphynx who'd summoned Julie in Qtana's hospital room bounced lithely out of the front seat on the prosecution's side and strolled over to the witness stand, then jumped onto the seat. The clerk of the court swore him in as he solemnly held one front paw in the air.

The court reporter approached the Sphynx. "Please spell your name for the record."

That took a hundred years. "Please refer to me as Horusiris," the Sphynx told the court. "Otherwise, we will be here all day."

Harrington walked up to the witness stand. "You lead the internal affairs division at the PMA. Is that correct?"

The Sphynx blinked. "Yes."

"Why are you uniquely suited for the role?" Harrington asked.

"Because I can read minds, so I know when someone is lying." The Sphynx glanced at Qbiit.

"Can you tell me about what happened on Monday morning at the PMA?" Harrington pressed.

"Yes. Captain Kaplan held a briefing in the auditorium for

people from the law enforcement and science divisions of the PMA. Afterward, we, the IA division, interviewed everyone."

"Was the defendant present for his interview?"

"No." The Sphynx smirked, showing very white teeth. "Qbiit was absent from work that day."

"Did you come across anyone else who appeared suspicious?" Harrington asked.

"*Appeared* suspicious?" The Sphynx sniffed. "Mr. Harrington, I didn't interview anyone who was even remotely involved with all this. I would have known if I had."

Harrington nodded. "I understand you have testimony from a witness who is medically incapable of attending the trial."

"Yes. Qtana, a troll."

Harrington turned to the judge. "I request the use of the memory orb, Your Honor."

The judge nodded. "Granted."

A tall, bearded man in long navy robes whom Julie hadn't noticed as he stood in the shadows near the clerk's seat stepped forward and held up his hands, muttering. With a soft *pop*, a huge orb appeared, hovering in the empty space between the attorneys' tables and the judge's bench. A murky silver substance floated inside it, and it shone like glass.

"The warlock of the court," Taylor explained softly, gesturing at the bearded man.

"Wonder if we can recruit him?" Julie mused.

Taylor rolled his eyes.

The warlock waved his hand at the Sphynx, still muttering, and Qtana's hospital room appeared in the orb. Qtana was in bed, and Julie was sitting in the chair beside her.

"Horusiris, please identify the individuals in your memory for the record," Harrington requested.

"The troll's name is Qtana. She works in the IT department of the PMA," the Sphynx told the court. "The little human is Julie Meadows, a PMA recruiter."

A rumble ran through the room. Julie shifted uncomfortably.

"Proceed." Harrington stepped back.

Julie found it weird to see her conversation with Qtana play out like a soap opera on the orb. She winced when she kept shrugging and waving the sandwiches.

"Do I really do that with my face when I'm annoyed?" she hissed.

Taylor smirked. "Adorably so."

She elbowed him in the ribs, and they both froze when Kaplan glared at them.

The memory ended with Qtana telling the Sphynx about Qbiit working with someone else. The orb went back to its swirly silver state, and Harrington turned to the judge. "Your Honor, I would like to have this memory marked as the Eternity Throne's Exhibit Number One, and I ask that it be admitted into evidence."

The judge looked at the trolls. "Does the defense have any objection?"

The troll lawyer glanced at Qbiit. Julie guessed he wanted to play the last part of Qtana's testimony in his favor. "No, Your Honor."

The memory was admitted, and Harrington turned to the Sphynx. "Thank you. No further questions."

"Does the defense have any questions?" the judge asked.

The Sphynx looked the troll lawyer dead in the eyes, then lifted a hind leg and enthusiastically began to lick his asshole.

The troll's cheeks turned scarlet. "No, Your Honor," he snarled.

Excused, the Sphynx leaped down from the stand and stalked back to his seat with his tail in the air. Julie gave him a thumbs-up as he jumped onto the bench beside hers.

Harrington called Kaplan to the stand, and the weretiger oozed menace as he was questioned. Some of his memories were sent into the orb too. Julie grimaced as she shrugged and waved her hands. She also watched through Kaplan's tiger eyes as he fought the group of Yetis in the Brooklyn sewer that had attacked her, Taylor, and Malcolm last week. The fear in the Yetis' eyes sent a shudder down her spine.

"Have you discussed the Yetis' muggings with their leadership?" Harrington asked.

Kaplan nodded. "I visited the Yetis' Lands shortly after Malcolm Nox was mugged."

Julie leaned forward and glanced at Taylor. "Did you know about this?" she whispered.

He shook his head.

Harrington paused. "What did the Yetis tell you?"

"Nothing. They wouldn't receive any visitors, and PMA policy has allowed them to exist independently for generations." Kaplan folded his arms. "I didn't kick their door down, and I hardly saw a single Yeti. The Ice Palace was sealed. The mountain was very quiet. I could smell Yeti activity, so I knew they were around, but they were far more skittish than they've ever been."

"Why do you think this was?" Harrington asked.

"Objection!" Qleb snapped. "Speculation."

"Sustained," the judge murmured. "Mr. Harrington, focus your questions on the facts."

"It's not speculation," Kaplan growled. "Those Yetis were scared. They didn't act like people who were trying to start a war. They acted like victims."

The judge's eyes met Kaplan's and narrowed. Julie couldn't help noticing that the corner of Kaplan's mouth twitched briefly.

"Keep your answers factual and relevant, Captain Kaplan," Judge Penelope ordered. "Mr. Harrington, continue your questioning."

There was muttering when Kaplan told Harrington about sending Julie and Taylor to find Malcolm Nox. Julie could feel the pressure of hundreds of eyes on her skin, and she squirmed in her seat.

Kaplan heard it and glared around at the courtroom. "Meadows and Woodskin will be key to unraveling this case," he snarled.

"What happened once Qbiit was returned to Headquarters?" Harrington pushed on, ignoring him.

"I interrogated him." Kaplan shot a glare at Qbiit.

The memory was sent into the orb, and Julie watched through Kaplan's eyes as Qbiit was brought into a small, windowless room and pushed into a chair behind a steel table. He sat down, eyes darting around. Kaplan strode up to him, grabbed the table, and moved it to one side. He pulled up a chair and sat inches from Qbiit, their knees almost touching.

"Okay, troll," Kaplan growled. "We've got you dead to rights. I don't need to ask you who mind-controlled those Yetis because I know you did, and I have Qtana's testimony to confirm it."

Qbiit snarled, "That bitch!"

"You mean the bitch who made your career?" Kaplan shot back. "The bitch who's been covering your ass since she came to the PMA? The bitch whose work you've been stealing since you discovered her brilliance, to flaunt it as your own and claim the credit?"

Qbiit's eyes narrowed. "She needed guidance."

"She needs a promotion and a raise," Kaplan barked. "And you need to never see the light of day again." He leaned closer, and Qbiit strained back as far into his chair as he could. "I don't need to ask if it was you who controlled those Yetis. I'm curious, though, as to why you used them for muggings. What did you need the money for?"

Qbiit looked away.

"I'm guessing it was for making the portals with the tech you stole from the PMA." Kaplan leaned back. "And for the techno-magical equipment you needed to expand your mind-control spell."

Qbiit sneered. "It's not like my government salary would cover more than room and board in Avalon Village."

"Oh, you want a raise, do you?" Kaplan spat. "I also know that you weren't acting alone. No troll could cast a spell like that."

"And no other species could use technology like that!" Qbiit yelled, lunging forward.

Kaplan didn't flinch. "Interesting how you're bragging about that, considering it wasn't your technology. It was Qtana's." He folded his arms. "Tell me, Qbiit. Who were you working with? Or, judging by the recent payments to your account, who were you working *for?*"

Qbiit ground his teeth. Flecks of foam appeared at the corners of his mouth, and he seemed to choke on his words.

"You're not helping yourself by clamming up," Kaplan growled. "Maybe this person coerced you. Maybe you didn't entirely know what was going on. That could lighten up some of the murder charges. Do yourself a favor and tell me what happened."

Julie glanced at the troll lawyer. He'd grown very pale, and he turned to Qbiit, whispering urgently. Qbiit didn't respond.

In the memory orb, Kaplan leaned closer to Qbiit. "We can protect you."

"I know," Qbiit growled bitterly.

"Then you know you're safe. Tell me who it is. I can keep you alive."

Qbiit's skin flushed and more foam collected on his lips, but he didn't utter a word. He shook his head vehemently.

"Fine. If that's how it's going to be." Kaplan sat up straight. "I tried to respect your rights, and I tried to offer you a deal. You won't give me the person who's behind all this, so the Sphynxes and the courts will get it from you." He stormed out of the room.

"Was this the only time you interrogated the defendant?" Harrington asked Kaplan.

"No." Kaplan folded huge arms. "I've been at him since we

caught him on Monday evening, but he hasn't spoken a word since then. He's not giving anything up."

Harrington had no further questions. When the judge asked Qbiit's lawyer if he wanted to question Kaplan, the weretiger let out another rumbling growl, and the troll shook his head.

"The witness is excused," the judge commanded.

Kaplan got up, and as he left the stand, the judge fixed Harrington with a sharp look. "The prosecution may call the next witness."

"The Eternity Throne calls the recruiter who arrested the defendant," Harrington responded. "Julia Meadows."

CHAPTER THIRTEEN

"Is that the human?" the Sylthana Elf yelled from the gallery.

Chaos erupted in the courtroom. The fae juror jumped to her feet and stared at Julie.

"She has no place here!" a Were shouted from the gallery.

"What's she doing in our world?" one of the reporters bellowed.

The winged lizard gave a raucous cry and madly flapped its wings, making the memory orb swing in the air. The warlock cursed and rushed forward, holding up his hands and chanting.

Qbiit's lawyer jumped to his feet. "Your Honor, I object!"

"On what grounds, Qleb?" the judge barked.

The troll paused, then gestured at Julie. "She's *human*!"

"I can find nothing in the law to prevent a human from giving testimony. She is a Para-Military Agency employee and eligible to testify." The judge looked at Julie. "Come to the stand, Miss Meadows."

"Objection!" Qleb shrieked.

"Denied!" the judge shouted. "And once again, I remind this courtroom that anyone who cannot behave will be held in contempt of court! Now, come to the stand at once!"

Julie froze on the bench.

"It's okay. Go on," Taylor whispered.

She sucked in a breath and got to her feet, then looked at Qbiit, remembering the awful wail Leafeyes' wife had uttered at the memorial. Fire roiled inside her. *You're going down, asshole*, she hissed in her mind as she strode up to the clerk of the court to be sworn in.

When she took the stand, Harrington turned to face her. The Were's eyes were unexpectedly kind. They had oblong pupils like a horse's, and he gave her a steady smile that made her fluttering heart slow down.

"How long have you been working for the Para-Military Agency?" he asked.

"Sir, I, uh..." Julie took a deep breath and looked into the soft brown eyes. "A few weeks, sir."

"Before you joined the PMA, did you know the paranormal world existed?"

"No, sir." Julie glanced at the gallery.

Harrington shifted his weight to draw her attention back to him. "How did you come to join the agency, then?"

"I was drafted, sir. I mean, fake-drafted. It was a ruse to get recruits in for a breakfast. Um, the IRSA 4000 sent me a draft notice by accident. That's the recruitment system used at the PMA, sir." Julie stammered to a halt.

Harrington smiled again. "When was the first time you had anything to do with Yetis?"

"The day I was drafted, sir. I went out for a drive, and I found Malcolm Nox wounded on the sidewalk after being mugged by a Yeti." Julie took a deep breath, and her heart slowed down more. "He was badly hurt."

Harrington walked her gently through the rest of the events, probing with subtle questions until the story flowed easily from her. The grumbles from the gallery faded as Julie got into the story. The memory orb was used to add to her testimony.

She forced herself to look at Harrington or Qbiit when she was nervous.

I'm going to get you, she growled at the troll in her mind.

Finally, Harrington talked her through the fight in the caverns, having her describe the circle in as much detail as she could.

"What happened when you broke the circle?" he prompted.

"The Yetis stopped fighting," Julie told him. "They looked like they were waking up. One who looked like their elder howled at them, and they all ran away." She felt a burst of heat behind her breastbone. "Some died in the fight. We had to kill some, and they were being used. They were forced to do it."

Harrington glanced at Qbiit. "Did you speak to the defendant during the fight?"

"Yes." Julie shot the troll a glare.

"What did he tell you about the circle?" Harrington pressed.

"He said that it was some of the greatest magic in the world and that most paranormals are too 'cowardly' to touch it." Julie wondered if air quotes were suitable in the courtroom and decided that they weren't. "He also talked about how he wanted to show the world that there was more to trolls than working in IT and more to politics than the seven royal families."

A murmur rushed through the courtroom. Qleb leaned closer to Qbiit, hissing in his ear. Qbiit gritted his teeth, his eyes meeting Julie's, and he slammed his cuffed fists on the table in anger.

"It looked to me like Qbiit was far from being coerced," Julie added, meeting his eyes with a challenging stare. "He was excited about his big plan."

Qbiit let out a low moan. A bailiff stepped forward.

"Ob—" Qleb began.

"There is nothing for you to object to, Qleb," Judge Penelope barked, cutting him off. "The witness is stating an observation."

"What happened after the Yetis left?" Harrington continued.

Julie paused, remembering the malevolence in Qbiit's reaction. "Qbiit tried to attack me with a syringe filled with Malcolm Nox's blood, but we subdued him."

Harrington gave the jury a pointed glance. "Qbiit attacked you *after* the circle was broken?"

"Yes." Julie hesitated. "It didn't look like the circle was affecting Qbiit."

Harrington stepped back. "Thank you. No further questions."

This time, when the judge asked Qleb if he had any questions, the troll flew to his feet. "I do, Your Honor." He strode up to Julie, eyes blazing behind his glasses. "What do you think you're doing here, *human*?"

Harrington flew to his feet. "Objection!" he thundered. "Discrimination!"

"Sustained," the judge snapped. "Qleb, unless you have a valid line of questioning for this witness, I suggest you immediately return to your seat."

Qleb's face twisted with hatred, but he strode back to the table, and Julie was excused. Her knees wobbled as she took her place and Taylor was called to the stand.

"Looked like you were about to shit yourself, Meadows," Kaplan hissed.

Julie shot him a glare.

The captain relented. "Testimony was fine. Relax."

Taylor leaned back on the stand, answering Harrington's questions in a smooth tone. The warlock cast his memories into the orb, and Julie watched the battles again. A murmur rose from the courtroom when they saw Julie diving for the circle and the Yetis scattering after it had been broken.

When Taylor slid back onto the bench beside Julie, she gave him a light punch on the arm. "Good job."

"Prince, remember?" Taylor shrugged. "We all had to learn public speaking, even though I'm sixth in line."

"That's it for the prosecution," Kaplan rumbled. "Let's see if Qbiit's tongue is a little looser now."

Harrington wasn't done. He turned to the courtroom again. "The Eternity Throne calls Randkluft to the stand."

Julie gasped. "What?"

Qleb spoke urgently to Qbiit, but the defendant said nothing as a familiar hulking form rose from its seat and strode to the stand. It was the tall, gray-tufted elder Yeti Julie remembered from the caverns. The warlock stepped forward and drew a rune on the Yeti's forehead with his staff, and when the clerk of the court swore him in, he stood still for a few seconds before answering with a garbled rumbling sound. A beat later, a disembodied mechanical voice spoke from above the Yeti's head. "I do."

Julie winced. "No wonder Qtana was working on a way to do this telepathically."

"Right?" Taylor mumbled.

The Yeti gave his name as Randkluft. He took his place on the stand, and Harrington stepped up to him. "Where are you from?"

He spoke in his gurgling language, and the disembodied voice translated to English. "The Yeti Lands in North Avalon."

"Have you ever met this troll?" Harrington pointed. "Let the record reflect that I'm pointing at the defendant."

Randkluft nodded, then remembered to say, "Yes."

"Where did that happen?" Harrington asked.

It was slow going, but the Yeti told his story methodically, his eyes darting around the room and resting for a few moments on Julie in a way that made her toes curl inside her boots. "I was on the mountainside, gathering pine nuts. The air opened, and the green one came forth from nothing. I offered him some pine nuts and shelter, for the air was bitter with the coming storm. He lifted a piece of glass and steel in his hand and thrust it into my arm. There was great pain, and I became a prisoner within my mind."

Julie's stomach twisted. She'd hoped the Yetis had been unconscious for the whole thing.

"What happened next?" Harrington prompted gently.

The Yeti's mouth drooped. "I was taken to the caverns. I did not want to be there. None of my people wanted to be there. There was a female green one and a blood drinker in a silver cage. The accused green one took blood from us and the blood drinker and threatened the female with violence. She had no choice. We had no choice. No one had a choice except the green one. It was not right."

Harrington took a step closer, spreading his hands. "Randkluft, did you ever hear the defendant talking to anyone apart from Qtana and Mr. Nox?"

"Yes. He was speaking to one who had power. One who was giving orders." Randkluft's nose wrinkled. "I smelled black magic. Its taint like rust in the air. The green one did not act alone."

"Do you know who this person is?" Harrington pressed.

The Yeti ignored him. He bunched his huge hands into fists and glared up at the judge. "You must put this right. My people did not ask for war or violence. My people are angry. They are hurt, and they are afraid.

"My people killed and were killed, as helpless as snowflakes on the wind. My people are bruised and battered because of what he has done. You must make it so the green one can hurt no one else, and then you must make it so my people will be left alone to live in peace as we did before the coming of the green one."

"Objection, Your Honor!" Qleb barked. "The answer is non-responsive."

"Sustained. That's enough, Randkluft," Judge Penelope rapped the gavel. "You are required to answer only the questions Mr. Harrington poses."

Randkluft let out a low, warbling sound of annoyance but lowered his hands to his sides. "No. I do not know who it was."

"No further questions, Your Honor." Harrington bowed to the judge.

Qleb asked to question the witness. Julie's fingernails bit into her palms as the troll approached Randkluft.

"You said you heard my client speaking to someone who was giving orders." Qleb had to lift his chin to look the Yeti in the eye. "Is that correct?"

"If it was not correct, I would not have said it," Randkluft rumbled.

"Did you have the impression that the person in question was in authority?"

"Yes."

"Did my client appear frightened by this unknown person?"

Randkluft's eyes drifted to Qbiit, then back to his lawyer, and his lips curled in a sneer that revealed the long yellow tusks in his bottom jaw. "He was afraid of his master in the way that a brave young Yeti fears the mountain he climbs to find a new story to sing to the one he loves. He was afraid, but he was determined to prove himself. He was not coerced. If anyone in this room knows what coercion is, I do."

"Objecti—" Qleb began.

"Denied," Judge Penelope snapped. "Do you have any further questions?"

Qleb bared his teeth. "No."

"I call a recess for fifteen minutes." The judge tapped the gavel.

Julie hadn't realized she was holding her breath until they walked out into the hallway. Taylor blew out his lips. "Stressful, huh?"

"I'm pretty sure Qleb wasn't listening to my testimony," Julie grumbled. "Qbiit wasn't being coerced. Didn't Qleb hear him ranting in my memory? I mean, come on!"

"It doesn't matter if Qleb heard," Taylor pointed out. "The case against Qbiit is ironclad. The jury's not going to buy Qleb's coercion angle."

"Not unless Qbiit makes a good defense for himself on the stand." Kaplan paced up and down the hall. "Or Qleb calls very credible witnesses."

"There won't be any." Julie sank into a chair, folding her arms. "We all know what he did. The question is who he was working for." She looked at Kaplan. "Do you have any ideas, sir?"

Kaplan shook his head. "All I know is that whoever it is, their goal is to cause even more political division than we already have."

"So, the Sylthana Elves," Taylor muttered darkly.

"What? Why?" Julie stared at him.

"You heard the elves in the gallery. They're determined to grab the Eternity Throne no matter what." Taylor folded his arms. "They haven't had a single candidate pass the test to establish worthiness for the Throne, but they're determined to discredit the Lunar Fae in every way they can, as well as anyone else who opposes their right to it."

"I see." Julie smirked. "No love lost between the Aether and Sylthana Elves."

"It's not about that. I don't care if I'm sixth in line to the Aether Throne or the Eternity Throne." Taylor shrugged. "I just know the Sylthana Elves are all troublemakers."

Julie thought about Dr. Olena. "I'm not so sure about that."

"I don't think Woodskin is wrong in thinking it must be someone from one of the royal families seeking to spread chaos." Kaplan gave a growling sigh. "But it's impossible to tell if it's the Sylthana Elves or some other family."

"Dr. Olena is one of the nicest, most humble people I've ever met." Julie tipped her chin up. "I can't imagine her being part of anything like this."

"Dr. Olena isn't from one of the high-ranking Sylthana families," Taylor explained. "She wouldn't benefit if a Sylthana Elf was on the Eternity Throne. It's distant to her, even more distant than it is to me."

Julie shrugged. "Okay. I'm still reserving judgment, though."

When they returned to the courtroom, Harrington was sitting at his table, going through notes. The Sphynx had stretched out on the bench to nap. When Julie scooted into her seat, he rolled onto his back and stretched, yawning and exposing an irresistibly wrinkly pink belly. Julie tickled it. The Sphynx purred.

Taylor and Kaplan stared at her. Kaplan's eyes were wide, which Julie had never seen happen. "What?" She held up her hands. "He's a cat."

"That is not just a *cat*," Kaplan hissed, but the tap of the gavel cut him off.

Judge Penelope leaned forward. "The defense may call its first witness."

Qleb rose. "I call the defendant."

Qbiit got to his feet but hesitated. He gave Qleb a long look, then his knees bent as though he would sit back down. Qleb whispered urgently to him, tugging at his arm, and Qbiit shuffled to the stand amid the clinking of chains, head hanging.

The troll took the stand, and Julie shifted in her seat, teeth clenched. "I'm ready to see the jury tear this asshole apart," she muttered.

"Shhh!" Taylor and Kaplan chorused.

Qbiit was sworn in, mumbling the words "I do" in a strangled whisper. He spelled his name for the clerk, then took his place on the stand.

Qleb stepped up to his client, casting a smirk toward the judge and the jury. "What is the nature of your work at the OPMA?"

Qbiit stared at him sullenly. He wouldn't say a word.

"Qbiit, I repeat. What is the nature of your work at the OPMA?" Qleb ground out.

Qbiit gazed across the courtroom, his eyes watery and unfocused. A muscle jumped in his cheek, but not a sound escaped him.

The Sphynx sat up very straight. "Oh, *my*," he whispered.

Qleb leaned closer. "Qbiit, answer the question."

Judge Penelope gripped her gavel. "Sir, answer your attorney's question."

"Mmm." Qbiit squeezed out the sound, then shook his head and stayed silent.

"Sir, I insist you answer the question, or you shall be considered in contempt of court and jailed!" The judge's voice echoed through the courtroom like a thunderclap.

The Sphynx jumped onto Harrington's table, scattering papers everywhere. "Your Honor, if I may?"

All eyes in the courtroom turned to him.

"What are you doing?" Harrington hissed.

"I do apologize for interrupting this rather drawn-out legal process of yours." The Sphynx sat on Harrington's paperwork. "But I think you should know that the defendant has been magically gagged with a dark geas. He couldn't say a word if he wanted to."

There was total silence. Kaplan was motionless. Julie glanced at his pale face. "Sir?"

"It shouldn't be possible," Kaplan snarled. "The courtroom is warded!"

"What does that—" Julie began.

Judge Penelope's forehead was studded with drops of sweat. Her voice was steady. "Warlock of the court, kindly remove the spell placed upon the defendant."

The warlock stepped forward, raising his arms. Qbiit's shoulders sagged and he leaned toward the warlock, closing his eyes. Placing gnarled hands on Qbiit's head, the warlock bowed his head for a second before speaking. "The Sphynx is right. The defendant is under a powerful dark spell."

Judge Penelope sat back in her seat, her eyes wide. Voices rose around the courtroom, gasping and muttering, and the judge had to tap her gavel twice for silence.

"Please continue," she intoned.

The warlock nodded. He cupped Qbiit's head in his hands again and began to chant in a low voice. Wisps of blue light curled around his fingers and sank through Qbiit's ears, and his chant reached a crescendo.

The troll's head exploded.

CHAPTER FOURTEEN

Shocked silence draped the courtroom. The warlock stepped back, stricken, staring down at his robes and hands, which were splattered with blood and grayish blobs of brain tissue. Judge Penelope was wiping blood from the front of her robe.

Julie felt something hot dripping down her face. She mopped it off with the sleeve of her jacket, and her stomach lurched. It was blood.

"Gross," she mumbled.

The leading Sylthana Elf sprang to the front of the gallery, pointing at Judge Penelope. "It's her!" he bellowed. "She tricked us! She's rigged the trial!"

"Nonsense!" Harrington thundered, leaping to his feet.

Qleb was wiping his bloody glasses on his suit jacket, then pointed them at the warlock. "What did you do?"

"Murderer! Murderer!" the Sylthana Elves chanted. "Murderer! Murderer!"

"It wasn't me!" the warlock gasped. "How could you not know your client was gagged? What have *you* done?"

"*Me?* This case was supposed to make my career! I had nothing to do with that!" Qleb shrieked.

The judge slammed her gavel down. "Order! I demand order in the court!"

Things had gone far beyond that. Qleb lunged and grabbed the warlock by the front of his bloody robes, yelling in his face. The bailiffs lumbered into the fray. Up in the gallery, the Sylthana Elves were chanting, "Lunar Fae are murderers! Lunar Fae are murderers!" and a Were plunged forward. "Don't insult my queen!" he roared and shoved the leader of the Sylthana Elves backward. The others surged forward, and the Sylthana Elf took a swing, knocking the Were sprawling.

"It was the human!" the warlock shrieked as the bailiffs dragged Qleb away from him. "She's the outsider. She's to blame!"

There was a yell from the jury, and a dwarf leaped out of the box and rushed at Julie. Kaplan casually clotheslined him, and he sprawled on the floor. He was holding his phone to his ear. "Backup at the courtroom!" he barked into it. "We need backup *now!*"

Julie wished she'd thought to bring her gun. She curled her hands into fists instead, aware of a battery of glares from the media side of the room. Randkluft got up and fled the courtroom, letting out a troubled moan. The Sylthana Elves pounded down from the public gallery, and the fight spilled over in front of the bench as they pushed toward the judge. A single bailiff stood in front of it with a dagger in each hand to defend her.

"We've got to stop them!" Julie shoved past Taylor.

"Julie, wait!" Taylor yelled.

Julie was halfway up the aisle. She grabbed a glass of water from Harrington's desk and flung it at the Sylthana Elf leader. It shattered on the back of his head and he roared, then spun, and his eyes fixed on Julie.

She raised clenched fists. "Come and get me, asshole!"

The courtroom doors banged open, and the steady thump of feet marching in unison announced the arrival of twenty blue-clad PMA soldiers. They parted seamlessly to go around Julie and surged into the group of Sylthana Elves. Taylor was suddenly beside her, and he grabbed her arm and dragged her back toward their seats. "Take it easy, Rocky."

"You've seen *Rocky?*" Julie raised her eyebrows but allowed herself to be towed away from the fight.

Taylor scoffed. "Who hasn't?"

Kaplan and the soldiers had the room under control in ten seconds flat. The Sphynx rubbed against Julie's knees, purring, as she watched the fighters being frog-marched out of the room. Harrington had a cut over his eye, and a cheerful medic appeared to whisk him away through a portal. The public gallery had magically cleared. The jury was hustled away, and Judge Penelope wearily declared a mistrial.

"Media. Out," Kaplan growled, standing at the courtroom doors.

"We have a right—" a dwarf reporter began.

"There's no trial here now. *Out,*" Kaplan snapped.

The media shuffled off, grumbling, and when Kaplan drew the doors shut, the room was almost empty. Only the Sphynx, Julie, Taylor, the judge, Kaplan, and the gory corpse of Qbiit slumped over the witness stand remained.

Judge Penelope came down from the bench, then pulled off her robes and draped them over one arm. She wore a black t-shirt and jeggings underneath. "Okay, Jack. What just happened?"

Kaplan shrugged, his enormous shoulders lending weight to the movement. "I was hoping you could tell me."

The judge sat on the edge of an attorney's table, staring at Qbiit's corpse.

"Sir, what does 'warded' mean?" Julie asked.

Kaplan arched an eyebrow at Taylor, then turned to Julie. "There's powerful magic on this courtroom to prevent the use of magic except the court warlock's, Meadows. It's to stop people from magically tampering with witnesses. Theoretically, what happened to Qbiit was impossible."

Julie's stomach lurched. "Unless whoever is responsible for the warding made a mistake."

"Or betrayed the Eternity Throne and the order and justice it stands for." Penelope sighed. "What are your instincts telling you, Jack?"

"Nothing other than the obvious. He had that geas on him before he was arrested. The question is, why didn't the wards pick it up both here and at OPMA? Whoever Qbiit is working for, they have strong dark magic, and they used it to kill him."

Julie ran a hand through her hair. "How are we going to catch them now?"

"I don't know yet." Kaplan's lip curled, and a snarl rumbled in his chest."But when I do, they're going to regret being born."

"How did you know that he was under a geas?" Judge Penelope asked the Sphynx.

He curled his tail around his paws and blinked. "I have to admit that it was not obvious even to me until the questions turned to his crimes. The captain is correct. Whoever placed the geas on Qbiit has a soul that will never be whole. Magic that dark comes at a great cost, and those who wield it pay a greater price to conceal their deviance."

"So basically, we have no idea who did it or how to find out," Julie muttered.

Kaplan shot her a glare. "No one asked for your opinion, Meadows."

The judge spread her hands. "She's not wrong."

Kaplan sighed and turned to Julie and Taylor. "There's nothing more for you to do here. Go back to HQ. Whatever's about to go down, I need my recruiters back on the job. We're going to need all the hands we can get."

Julie's eyelids felt like they'd been tied down with lead weights. As she followed Taylor through the portal back into Central Park, she half-expected to see a star-strewn night sky above her. Instead, when the portal spun them out of Avalon onto the grubby footpath, it was still daylight. Traffic crawled bumper-to-bumper along the street, a mass of shining, honking metal. The park rang with voices. Somewhere, an overtired toddler was pitching a huge tantrum. Julie knew how he felt.

"I'm so tired." She rubbed her cheeks.

It was the first time either had spoken since they'd left the courthouse. Taylor gave her a wan smile. "It's been a long-ass day."

"Court was..." Julie puffed out her cheeks. "'Intense' is one word for it."

"I don't *have* words for it," Taylor mumbled.

Julie paused before stepping out from under the bridge. She glanced down at her clothes, still streaked with dried blood. "We're going to get arrested, walking the streets like this."

"Oh, don't worry. No one will see it." Taylor touched one of his pointed ears. "Every part of a paranormal's body, alive or dead, is hidden by the standard illusion we all have to protect ourselves from humans. We'll look like we're spattered with mud to human eyes."

Silence fell over them again as they crossed the street at the light, ignoring the empty-eyed glowers of the drivers in the front row, and headed into the welcome shade and peace of the parking garage. Randkluft's voice kept ringing in Julie's head. *My people killed and were killed, as helpless as snowflakes on the wind.* She had only known Yetis as mindless, wordless, violent beasts, but Randkluft's expressive eyes and smooth voice? She couldn't forget them. She couldn't forget the way it had sounded in the cavern when the stalactite crashed down on them.

She hadn't had a choice, but it still sat in her chest like a cannonball.

Genevieve's sleek black-and-pewter lines came into sight, and Julie let out a long breath. Taylor glanced at her as they approached the car. "You okay?"

"Yeah." Julie mustered a smile. "Just glad to see Genevieve."

Taylor ran a hand through his hair. "I can't stop seeing Qbiit's head." A shudder ran through him. "The bits of *brain*."

Julie didn't know what to say, so she patted him on the shoulder and unlocked Genevieve's door.

Finally! Hat was sitting on the center console in his Panama form. *What took you so... Why are you covered in blood?*

Julie winced at the screech of his voice in her head. She slid into the driver's seat. *Not ours.*

Taylor flopped into the passenger seat and slammed the door. Grasping the wheel, Julie squeezed it between her fingers a few times, then turned to him. "Taylor, what the *hell* just happened?"

"Apart from Qbiit's head exploding?" Taylor sighed.

"I don't mean that. I mean *everything* that went on in that courtroom." Julie waved her hands. "The tension, the fighting—"

"Fighting?" Hat spluttered.

Taylor shook his head and sank back. "I don't have answers, Julie. I don't."

Julie felt a nudge at the edge of her consciousness, like an intrusive thought. Hat was searching her mind for answers. She closed her eyes and allowed herself to replay the events in her mind for the hundredth time since leaving the courthouse.

"Oh, dear," Hat murmured when she remembered the Sylthana Elves' protest about Judge Penelope. Then, "Oh, no!" as she thought about the uproar when she'd been called to the stand. Finally, when she relived Qbiit's heat exploding, Hat exclaimed, "Oh, *my*!"

"Tell me court's not always like this, Hat," Taylor begged.

"It usually isn't, but I fear it will be like this for the next handful of years." Hat's brim drooped.

Julie stared at him. "Handful of years? I would think decades since the Queen's still going to be around for a long time."

There was a long silence. Hat squirmed on the console, then straightened. "It's time you both learned about the real misfortune that has befallen the Eternal Throne."

Taylor's brow furrowed. "What, that there are no Lunar Fae left to take the Throne? I'm well aware of the succession problem, Hat. It's all my parents have talked about for my entire life."

"You only know what the Throne has allowed to become public knowledge," Hat retorted. "There's more to it than that."

"What do you mean?" Julie clenched the steering wheel tightly.

"You've been told that Queen Esmerelda has no heirs because the Lunar Fae are dying out." Hat shuffled on the console, getting comfortable. "What you don't know is how quickly this is happening and that the royals aren't the only ones."

Taylor frowned. "I know one of the Lunar Fae princesses was stillborn. It was sad. I was really young, but Mom and Dad took me to the funeral. I remember looking up at the picture of the baby and thinking how unfair it seemed. And we all know about the abdications."

"Abdications?" Julie asked.

"Yeah, two of the Lunar Fae abdicated. It was a scandal, really. I was a teenager then." Taylor sighed. "All this political tension is their fault."

"Not necessarily," Hat growled. "I'd blame whoever is responsible for the deaths."

"Deaths?" Taylor raised his eyebrows.

A chill crept down Julie's spine.

Hat paused. "Originally, there were nine princesses in Queen Esmerelda's family, all eligible to take the Throne."

"Nine?" Taylor gasped. "I only know about five. The two who abdicated, Charmaine who went missing in battle, Freya who disappeared at sea, and the stillborn one."

"Yes." Hat sighed. "As is custom, Lunar Fae heirs are only made public knowledge when they come of age. It's to protect the younger heirs. Of course, it's been public knowledge for a while that there *are* no younger heirs. Charmaine and Freya were both adults when they vanished, and it is customary to have public state funerals for any deceased princess. However, that custom was ignored three times."

"Hold up." Julie held out a hand. "Charmaine and Freya *vanished?*"

"Presumed dead, but the bodies were never found." Hat sighed. "Charmaine's death seemed almost inevitable. She was a warrior princess, if ever there was one, but people got suspicious after Freya died. When three more princesses were lost while they were underage, the Lunar Fae kept it quiet."

"Lost?" Julie's voice shook. It was difficult to picture anyone living in the Eternal Palace, but she couldn't help feeling for a family that had lost eight children. How did you live with that? Her family had lost one member, her dad, and it felt like the world had not been the same since.

Hat's crown dipped in a nod. "Two young princesses died during puberty from a magical illness. The third was only ten years old. She went out riding with her governess, and neither of them came back. It was a huge operation in the PMA long before either of you two joined. You would have just been kids back then. It was top secret. We never found her." His voice dropped an octave at the word "we."

Taylor blew out his cheeks.

"Well, *that's* not suspicious," Julie muttered. "How can *eight* princesses disappear?"

"That's the question," Hat agreed. "There's more than that, too. In the past two hundred years, which isn't that long in fae terms, three royal advisers have gone missing under very questionable circumstances."

Taylor sat up straighter. "I think I remember one of them.

Jehoahaz. The official statement was that he resigned without warning, but no one ever heard from him again."

"That's right." Hat nodded. "He's gone."

Julie let her hands slip off Genevieve's wheel and into her lap. "It's a lot to take in."

"There's something else." Hat hesitated. "Something only the highest-ranking members of the seven royal families know."

Taylor stared at him. "What?"

Hat hesitated, then his words came out in a rush. "The queen is dying."

"Dying!" Taylor sat bolt upright.

"Everyone kept telling *me* she was just getting tired and older." Julie let out a breath. "I'm guessing there are not decades left anymore."

"A few years if we're lucky. A blink of an eye in the life of a Lunar Fae." Hat's crown quivered. "If no successor is found before she dies, the paranormal world will be plunged into chaos."

"Dramatic," Julie commented.

Hat sighed. "Fine. There will be a civil war and not the kind where two sides fight each other. The whole world could fragment. It might be the end of the Eternity Throne, the end of a united paranormal world, the end of the PMA, and the end of stability. It'd be like medieval Europe but with black magic and dragon fire."

Taylor swallowed hard. "Ilsa."

Julie looked at him.

"My sister, remember? This paints a target on her back." Taylor sighed. "She's next in line for the Aether Throne, and she's the member of the Aether family who's eligible to take the test to determine if she's worthy of becoming the heir to the Eternity Throne."

Julie raised an eyebrow. He'd said "the test" like Ilsa would face a firing squad. "What test?"

"No one knows." Taylor sighed. "Those who have taken the test are under a geas never to talk about it."

Geas, Julie's orb training stepped in. *Unbreakable magical oath.*

"Sounds hectic." Julie grimaced. "I'm sorry. She seems cool."

"She's the best," Taylor mumbled, staring at his feet.

Julie's ringtone ripped through the air, and adrenaline scorched her veins. Taylor jumped, and Hat almost pitched off the center console. Laughing shakily, Julie fished her phone out of her pocket. It was an unknown number.

"Ugh, probably spam." Her finger hovered over the decline button.

"Wait!" Hat gasped. "I... Julie, you're going to want to take this one."

"What? Why?" Julie stared at him.

Hat's crown sagged. "Just trust me."

"Okay." Julie frowned. "You're being weird, but whatever." She swiped to answer and held the phone to her ear. "Um, hello?"

"Is this Julie Meadows?" The voice was cool and competent.

Julie scowled at Hat. "Spam," she mouthed, then, "Yes, that's me."

"I'm calling from Maimonides Midwood Community Hospital."

Julie's heart thudded. Where was that? Was it Mom? "What's happened?" she blurted.

"You are listed as the next of kin for a critically ill patient who was recently brought in by ambulance," the competent voice told her.

Julie felt the air crack like glass. Her breaths wouldn't come. She clutched her phone, her palm slippery with sweat, and struggled to squeeze out one of the thousand questions clashing in her mind. Her mouth opened and shut, but there was no sound.

"Julie?" Taylor whispered. "What's wrong? You've gone pale."

"Who?" Julie finally croaked out.

"Ms. Lillie Griswall."

Julie felt the world lurch under her. She clutched Genevieve's wheel for support. "What happened?"

"Ms. Griswall collapsed in her front yard, ma'am. Her neighbor called 911, and our ambulance was first on the scene. She gave your number as Ms. Griswall's next of kin."

"Collapsed!" Julie sucked in a breath. "What's wrong with her? Is she going to be okay?"

The competent voice hesitated for a beat that told Julie everything. "Our emergency physicians are working on her right now, but Ms. Griswall is in critical condition."

Julie closed her eyes, aware that she was trembling so hard that her phone tapped uncomfortably against her face. "Okay," she whispered. "I'm coming."

She lowered the phone. Taylor stared at her. "What's wrong?"

"It's Lillie," Julie croaked out. "She's in the hospital. She's—" Tears flooded her eyes. "It's not looking good, Taylor."

Taylor didn't reach out to touch her shoulder or offer comforting words. Instead, he grabbed Hat. "Turn into an emergency light," he barked. "Now! Julie, start the car. We're going to the hospital!"

Taylor's words ran through her like an electric shock, restarting her heart. She turned the key and stomped on the accelerator, and Genevieve responded with a guttural full-throated roar that Julie had never heard before. They peeled out of the parking garage and onto the crowded street with screaming tires.

CHAPTER FIFTEEN

Taylor wound down the window. He was holding a flashing bright red emergency light, and he slapped it on the roof.

Go, Julie, go! Hat shouted.

Julie gunned it. Seeing the light, cars gave way, and Julie wove around them until they reached the blessed expanse of the freeway. Traffic wasn't at its peak yet, and there was enough space to squeeze the roaring Mustang between the cars.

Julie slipped into the fast lane and stomped down with all her strength. Her engine reaching a high-pitched whine, Genevieve surged forward with a force that slammed Julie back in her seat. She gripped the wheel and changed gears, and somehow the car found even more speed. Julie glanced at the speedometer as it hovered around ninety and resolved not to look again. She locked her eyes on the road.

It was as though Genevieve knew what was happening. The car responded to the tiniest touch on the wheel or the accelerator. Cars slipped out of the fast lane in response to the emergency light, and Julie's world was suddenly blazing with brake lights. She stomped down hard as a sedan in front of her slammed on the brakes and swerved left and right as though panicking about where to go in the face of the emergency lights.

There was a space on the right, and Julie sucked in a breath and spun the wheel. Smooth as butter, Genevieve slipped into the next lane, and they cruised around the car despite their speed, then nosed back into the fast lane and accelerated again.

"Good girl, Genny," Julie panted. "Good girl!"

Taylor was clutching the handle over the door. "Oh, *shit.*"

"What?" Julie threw Genevieve down the next exit, following her GPS, and squealed onto an open road. She gunned it, and Genevieve responded as though she'd been waiting for this moment for weeks, surging forth at a speed that made Julie tremble.

"Lights," Taylor muttered.

"Lights? What do you—"

The yip of a siren cut Julie off short. She glanced in the rearview mirror at the police cruiser several hundred yards behind, struggling to keep up with the charging Mustang.

"Shit!" Julie yelled.

"Stop. Just stop," Taylor gasped. "Otherwise, they'll chase you, and it'll slow us down even more."

Julie knew he was right, but it still took every ounce of her willpower to lift her foot off the accelerator and ease Genevieve to the side of the road. The engine snarled, hungry for more, as Julie watched the cop get out of the car. Her heart sank. Was there a prison sentence for going this fast? Had she done a hundred or a hundred and ten in a sixty? Her stomach felt like it was filled with rocks.

Julie, show him your PMA ID, Hat hissed.

What? Why? Julie opened the glovebox and took out her license and registration as though that would help.

Forget the other paperwork. Just do it! Hat barked.

Julie fished her badge out of her pocket as the cop reached her window and tapped on it. She wound it down slowly, knowing what he would think about a speeding Mustang containing two youngsters splattered with mud. Her ID looked like it came from an insurance company to human eyes.

The cop was red-faced and panting. Julie wondered how long he'd been struggling to catch up with Genevieve. "Ma'am, do you know how fast you were going?" he snapped.

"Um—" Julie began.

Show him! Hat yelled.

She stuck out her arm, flashing her ID. "Official business," she blurted.

The cop's eyes widened. "FBI? Ma'am, I'm sorry."

"I need to get to the Maimonides Hospital right away." Julie clenched the ID tightly. "It's an emergency."

"Top secret," Taylor added.

The cop nodded. "You go, ma'am. I'll escort you so you don't run into any more trouble on the way." He glanced at Genevieve, his lip twitching. "If I can keep up, that is."

As soon as Julie heard the peal of the siren, she pulled back onto the road and floored it. As Genevieve plunged onto the road, she realized how little of the Mustang's strength she'd ever used. Genevieve's power seemed limitless. She ate up the distance in a matter of seconds, tires screaming as Julie turned down another side street, the cruiser frantically yipping behind them.

It seemed to take an eternity to push through the splitting traffic and reach the hospital, and as Genevieve screeched through the gate, Julie's head whipped left and right. There weren't any available spots.

"Shit!" she barked.

"You go. Go!" Taylor reached for the emergency brake. "I'll park Genevieve."

"Thanks," Julie replied. She shifted the car out of gear and flung out, then ran to the front doors. They parted, and for an instant, Julie expected to see Dr. Olena walk up to her. Instead, a petite Asian nurse sat behind the reception counter, typing on a computer.

Julie ran up to her. "Griswall. Lillie Griswall. Where is she?"

The nurse blinked at her. "You must be Miss Meadows?"

"Yes. Where's Lillie?" Julie's voice cracked.

"Just a minute, ma'am. Let me talk to her doctors and find out if she's still in the ER." The nurse reached for the phone.

Julie's eyes stung with tears. She pressed her fingers into her hair, squeezing, the faint pain of the pulling roots distracting her from the way her heart felt like it was going to crack her ribs open.

Running feet and heavy breathing announced Taylor's arrival. He was sweating as he held out Hat and Genevieve's keys. "Thanks," Julie mumbled, taking both.

"I got you." Taylor touched her shoulder with his fingertips.

The nurse put the phone down. "Miss… It's Julia, isn't it?"

"Julie." Julie swallowed. "Where's Lillie?"

"Lillie's stable for now." The nurse smiled as though Julie would know what that meant. "She's been taken to the ICU. It's not visiting hours, but…" She paused. "Since Lillie's just been brought in, you may be able to see her."

"Please." Julie's voice shook.

The nurse gave them the room number, and Julie barely resisted the urge to jog to the elevator. She walked as fast as she dared, with Taylor striding beside her. Her hands trembled as she hit the button for the ICU floor.

As the elevator began to move, Taylor leaned toward her, bumping her lightly with his shoulder. "Hey, don't worry so much. Lillie will be okay. She's a tough old bird; you know that. She's not going to let this get her down."

Julie fished out a faint smile, but her mind was replaying a horrified loop of memories from the past few weeks. Lillie telling her that there was a casserole in the oven when Julie knew nothing was cooking. Lillie asleep on the couch at five-thirty in the afternoon when Julie got home. Lillie forgetting the back door was open, so her little dog Pookie ran into the street. Lillie only eating one piece of pizza and watching *Fast & Furious* with only one or two hollers of excitement.

She pressed the heels of her hands into her temples. *Stupid, stupid, stupid!* How could she have failed to realize that Lillie was getting sick?

It's not your fault, Hat murmured. *Lillie could have told you.*

Lillie doesn't always know what she's thinking. Julie squeezed her eyes shut to hold back tears. *Oh, Lillie!*

Taylor's hand was on her shoulder. "Julie?"

"Sorry." Julie lowered her hands. "Sorry." The elevator doors were open, and she stumbled out and to the reception desk at the ICU ward.

I'll do the FBI thing to your ID again if I need to, Hat offered.

The nurse at the desk was welcoming when Julie explained that she was Lillie's next of kin or the closest thing. "It's not visiting hours, but Dr. Haynes will speak to you, and I'll take you to see her briefly."

"Thanks," Julie stammered.

The doctor was a suave, surprisingly young man with a stubbly beard, flipping through clipboards in a nearby hallway. He flashed his dimpled smile at Julie as the nurse led her up to him. "You must be Miss Meadows. Let me guess, a granddaughter?"

"No, I-I'm her tenant, but I guess she's..." Julie's throat closed.

Taylor took a step closer. "Julie is the closest thing Lillie has to family."

Dr. Haynes nodded. "Lillie is stable for now, but she's in poor condition. She was brought in just in time, and she's very weak from pneumonia."

Pneumonia! How could I not have known? Julie raged. She croaked, "Is she going to be okay?"

Dr. Haynes' dimples flashed again. "Given time and care, she has an excellent chance. She's in a private room, thanks to her insurance. I'll take you to her."

He showed her to a featureless white door in a small waiting room lined with them, but before he could take her inside, his pager beeped. He cursed and trotted off. She touched the cold metal of the handle and froze.

"Do you want me to come in with you?" Taylor asked softly.

Julie gently pulled Hat off her head and placed him in Taylor's hands. "No," she whispered. She mustered her courage, pushed the door open, and stepped into the room.

It was nothing like Qtana's. Here, everything was cold and bare. White tiles on the floor, the walls painted pale gray, and the bed in the middle of the floor was blue and white. Among it all, the woman Julie loved like a grandmother should have been a burning firebrand of color, but Lillie's face was ashen and waxy against her white pillow. Her eyes were closed, and she was surrounded by a mass of tubes and wires and masks and needles. She looked puny in that huge bed, shriveled among the hard lines of the monitors surrounding her. Her hair was a messy cloud around her face.

The door swung shut with a click. Lillie's eyes snapped open, and at last, there was a little color in the room. Behind the plastic mask over her face, her lips twitched. "Julie," she wheezed out.

The tears made a hot trail down Julie's cheek. She batted them away and ran across the room. She wanted to wrap her arms around Lillie, but she was scared to disturb the tubes and things. Instead, she crouched on the floor, grabbed Lillie's hand, and clutched it tightly, pressing her forehead against the old lady's worn and wrinkled knuckles.

"Easy, dear," Lillie rasped. Her sentences were broken up by long, rattling breaths. "Takes more...than...pneumonia to...get me down." She attempted a chuckle that sounded like sandpaper in her throat and coughed.

"I'm so sorry, Lillie," Julie choked. "I should have taken better care of you."

Lillie shook her head, then winced. "No, dear."

"I should have known you were sick. I was so busy..." Julie blinked against her tears, thinking about the handfasting. Why had she gone out to party instead of staying home with Lillie?

Lillie reached over with her other hand, patting Julie's weakly. "Shhh, dear. You have...a life of your own...to lead."

"I should have been home with you more often." Julie swallowed hard. "I don't think I've sat with you for a movie since I left on that work trip." That had been a week ago. Plenty of time for an elderly lady to get this sick. Had she even eaten the dinners Julie had cooked and put in the freezer for her?

"Don't be silly." Lillie gave her hand a feeble squeeze. "You do...more than enough...for me. More than my own...family has ever...thought to do."

"You *are* family to me," Julie whispered.

Lillie said nothing. The old lady's eyes had fluttered closed again. Julie glanced at the monitor, but it still calmly traced Lillie's heartbeat, and she let out a breath.

Not letting go of Lillie's hand, she glanced around for a chair. There was an uncomfortable plastic one within reach. Drawing it closer, Julie sank into it, wrapped both hands around Lillie's, and held on tight.

The squeak of the chair on the floor made Lillie's eyes flutter open again. She cleared her throat, a raw sound, and her fingers moved in Julie's grasp. "Thank you...for being here."

"Where else would I be?" Julie managed a smile. "I'm not leaving your side. Okay?"

Lillie's lips only twitched, but her eyes brightened.

"Rest, Lillie." Julie adjusted the sheet over the older woman's chest and smoothed a stray hair out of her eyes. "Just rest. I'll be here when you wake up."

"Okay," Lillie murmured, and her eyes closed again.

The chair grew progressively more uncomfortable as the hours slid by. Julie shifted for the tenth time in the past two minutes, trying to ease the pressure that was making her left foot go numb. Her hand was sweaty where it held Lillie's, but she didn't let go.

The old lady stirred. Julie froze. Lillie had been sleeping soundly for the past hour, and when Dr. Haynes had made his rounds shortly before that, he'd told Julie that rest was the best thing for her now. She held still until Lillie's breathing slowed again, then let out her breath and flexed her foot to dispel the pins and needles flooding it.

There was a quiet knock on the door. Julie looked up, expecting one of Lillie's nurses to check on her oxygen and IV fluids again. When the door opened, it was Taylor, wearing Hat as a stylish cloth cap. He was still in the suit he'd worn for court.

"Hey," Julie whispered. "What are you doing here? It's been hours."

"I picked up dinner from the gyro place outside." Taylor glanced at Lillie. "How is she?"

"Resting." Julie squirmed in her seat again.

"Think you can come out into the waiting room for some dinner? We'll be able to hear her from there if she wakes up."

Julie gave her landlady a long look. She seemed peaceful, her breathing slow and deep, even with the damp rattle.

"You need to keep your strength up. The cafeteria was closed, so I got you a chicken gyro." Taylor held up a greasy paper bag, smiling softly in that way that made his eyes crinkle.

Julie smiled too. It was her favorite street-food dinner. "Okay."

She reluctantly allowed Lillie's hand to slip out of hers and followed him out of the room. There were two considerably more comfortable chairs there, arranged around a small table.

Julie sank into one, watching apathetically as Taylor opened the paper bag and fished out two gyros and a heaping box of Greek fries.

When Julie unwrapped her gyro, she realized how hungry she was. Had she finished her sandwich at lunch? It felt like a thousand years ago. She bit into the gyro and sighed as her mouth filled with tzatziki.

"Have some fries, too." Taylor pushed the box closer to her.

Are you okay? Hat asked in her mind.

She glanced from Taylor's smile to the cap, then focused her attention on the gyro. *I'll be okay if Lillie's okay.*

"Want a soda?" Taylor asked. He rummaged in the paper bag. "I've got Coke and a Dr. Pepper. I wasn't sure what mood you were in today."

"Coke, please." Julie accepted it and took a deep gulp before she met Taylor's eyes. "Thanks, Taylor. I forgot about dinner."

Taylor grinned. "I figured as much. Is there anything else you need? Something I can get you from home? A ride?"

Julie shook her head. "I'm staying here for the night. Dr. Haynes said it was okay since Lillie's in a private room." She grimaced. "I never got back to the PMA. I bet Kaplan's spitting fire."

"Don't worry. I talked to him. He knows what's going on, and he says you should take a personal day tomorrow." Taylor took another bite of his gyro.

Julie let out a breath. "Thanks." She looked at the box of fries and took one but didn't eat it, just held it in midair. "Taylor, she was sick, and I didn't even know."

Her voice cracked, and Taylor looked at her. "I'm sure she doesn't blame you, Julie."

"Of course she doesn't, but *I* blame myself." Julie's eyes glazed with tears, and she put the fry back into the box. "Lillie's much more than my landlady. She's the grandma I never knew. She's always looking out for me, and she's always in my corner, and I can't believe she's in the hospital." She pressed the heels of her hands into her temples to force back her tears, taking deep breaths.

"You heard Dr. Haynes," Taylor murmured. "Lillie will be okay, and you're taking great care of her. You've been busy and hurt, Julie. You were laid up with a concussion just a few days ago, remember?"

She lowered her hands, and Taylor smiled. "This isn't your fault. I've heard you talk about the dinners you make for her and the time you spend together."

"It doesn't matter whose fault it is," Julie mumbled. "All that matters is that she gets better. I hate seeing her like this." She blinked hard. "So helpless and frail."

"I can only imagine how scary this whole day has been." Taylor sighed. "I'm sorry."

"It's been horrible." Julie shook her head. "I just keep thinking about when we went to the hospital after my dad was hit by a car. Everyone told me not to worry, but I *did* worry, and that evening, he died."

"I'm sorry," Taylor murmured. "It's okay to worry. Lillie will be okay, though. Everything's going to be fine."

She finished her gyro and most of the fries, then curled up on the chair, propping her chin on her hand. "Thanks. I needed that."

"I could tell you were heading toward hangry." Taylor gathered the empty wrappers and tossed them into the paper bag.

Julie scoffed. "I'm never hangry."

He raised an eyebrow. "Uh-huh. Sure you're not."

"I'm not!" Julie laughed.

Taylor put the trash in a nearby garbage can and flopped into the chair beside hers. "You going back inside?"

"In a minute. I don't want to wake her if she's sleeping well." Julie stifled a yawn. "What time is it, anyway?"

Taylor glanced at his phone. "Just past eleven."

"Wow." She yawned this time.

Taylor shifted, making himself comfortable in his chair, and opened a social media app. The first thing that popped up was a video of a big, burly dude hugging a group of baby goats that queued up for attention.

"Aw, look at them." Julie sighed.

Taylor chuckled. "Quit looking over my shoulder."

She ignored him, and he scrolled to the next video, which showed a baby goat jumping on a trampoline. Julie giggled. "Why is your social media full of goats?"

"Goats are awesome, okay?" Taylor retorted.

Her head was heavy. She let it rest on his shoulder as they watched a video of a herd of baby goats running through a barn door to be bottle-fed, but before the end of the video, her eyes fluttered closed. She barely noticed when Taylor gently draped an arm around her shoulders.

CHAPTER SIXTEEN

Julie straightened the throw on the couch for the hundredth time. Early morning light filled the living room through its lace curtains, and Julie stepped back, inspecting it. The coffee table was clean, and she'd opened the animal photography book to Lillie's favorite page. Random clutter littered most of the bookshelves, but she'd vacuumed the carpet and plumped the couch cushions.

She picked up a cloth and turned to the pictures arranged in the TV cabinet. After spritzing the glass frame of a photo showing two identical young girls leaning on a bridge railing, Julie gently wiped the glass clean.

"Your cleaning efforts are admirable, but don't you want to take the opportunity to declutter?" Hat asked from his perch on the arm of the sofa. He was an obnoxious burgundy ten-gallon hat today because Julie had asked if he could turn into something useful like a feather duster.

"I'm not going to go through Lillie's stuff just because she's in the hospital." Julie gave the frame a last polish. "I don't want her home to feel different when she gets here this afternoon. It's her space. She needs to feel cozy and comfy in it."

Hat sniffed. "Maybe you should have left it smelling vaguely of old cheese, then."

"Really? You're going to snark about that?" Julie grumbled. "I wasn't going to leave her fridge untouched after she'd been out for a week. That reminds me." She scooped up her cleaning supplies and dumped them into a basket on the coffee table. "I want to restock the fridge before she gets home. Feel like a trip to the grocery store?"

"Not if you're going to ask me to turn into something useful like a grocery basket," Hat retorted.

Julie groaned. "Quit being an ass." She grabbed the basket and hurried into the kitchen, then fished a notepad and a pen out of a drawer.

Hat hopped down from the sofa and waddled into the kitchen on his brim. He hopped onto one of the chairs as Julie scribbled a list. "Milk, chamomile tea, cookies." Julie ran a hand through her hair, then let out a breath through her lips. "What's she going to have for lunch tomorrow? I can fix her breakfast before I go to work and dinner when I get home, but she needs something easy for lunch. A sandwich. No, she hates sandwiches."

"Soup?" Hat suggested.

"I don't know. I don't think she's strong enough to heat things on the stove yet." Julie bit her lip. "A nice chicken salad. She doesn't mind salads. Something with chili in it." Julie scribbled. "Oh, and I need a non-slip mat for the bathroom. Hat, what if she falls while I'm not home? What if she ends up lying here for hours with no one to see her?"

"You'd think her family would help," Hat grumbled.

Julie sighed. "She doesn't talk about them, and if I was listed as her next of kin, I doubt she has anyone left. I'm her family now." She bit her lip. "Maybe I can leave a little later in the mornings. I'd have to skip training with Taylor, but I won't leave Lillie alone for a whole day. I'll also have to start leaving at five. No more overtime."

Hat winced. "With Kaplan putting more pressure on you?"

"It's not going to be easy," Julie admitted. "But Lillie's got to come first for a little while."

Her phone rang and Julie grabbed it, her heart jumping into her throat as it had done every time she heard it ring since Lillie collapsed. But it wasn't the hospital. It was her mom. She groaned, debating about declining the call. She was too busy to listen to thirty minutes of conspiracy theories right now.

Instead, she swiped at the screen and raised the phone to her ear. "Hey, Mom."

"*JULIAAAAAAAAAAAA!*" Rosa sang.

Julie winced and held the phone further away. "Hey."

"How are you, baby?" she trilled. "Are you excited to have Lillie home?"

"Yeah." Julie sighed. "I can't wait. This place feels wrong without her."

Pookie jumped onto a chair near Julie. Her tail wagged frantically as Julie rumpled her ears.

"You sound tired, baby. What's the matter?"

Julie sank into the chair beside Pookie. "I'm stressed out."

"Oh, you poor thing! You're probably suffering from a magnesium deficiency. Do you have any avocado oil pills? Those will *definitely* help."

Julie gritted her teeth. "Mom, I'm stressed out because I have to juggle pressure at work with looking after Lillie, and I'm leaving poor Lillie home alone all day every day this week when she's fresh out of the hospital." Her gut twisted. What if she missed something again?

Rosa wasn't listening. "Your digestion will be impacted, honey. Do you know what you need?"

"A million dollars and a live-in carer for Lillie?" Julie quipped.

"A natural colon cleanse!" Rosa cried. "I have some aloe vera concentrate that will blow you right open!"

Julie groaned and sagged back into her chair. "Pretty sure this is one problem that can't be solved by aloe vera juice, Mom."

"Oh, I know that. Don't you worry, sweet baby. Momma's got you." Mom chuckled. "I'll be there later today."

Julie's eyes snapped open. "You'll be... Wha—"

Rosa cheerfully bulldozed through her consternation. "Lillie needs someone to take care of her while you're at work, right?"

"Yeah, but—"

"Then it's settled." Rosa sighed with contentment. "I'll get packing."

"Packing?" Julie squawked.

"Mmhmm." She chuckled. "Getting the bus back and forth every day isn't doable, honey."

Julie's eyes widened in horror. "Wait, you don't mean—"

"I'll stay with you until Lillie is better!" Rosa continued brightly.

Julie curled into a ball. "Kill me now," she muttered.

"What was that?"

"Nothing!" Julie sighed. "Actually, Mom, thanks. That will really be helpful. I was terrified of leaving Lillie on her own after everything that happened."

"It's nothing, baby. Anything for my sweet child," Rosa cooed. "Now, what do you want me to bring for you? Avocado oil pills, aloe vera concentrate... Oooh, you know what's an excellent natural tonic?"

"No, but I'm pretty sure I'm about to hear about it," Julie mumbled.

"Cultured whey!" Rosa crowed.

Julie gagged. "Sounds disgusting."

"Oh, honey, it has the most amazing benefits," her mother gushed. "It boosts the immune system, it purifies the blood..."

Julie was pretty sure the idea of purifying the blood had left modern medicine along with the leeches, but she stretched out in her chair and let Mom's chatter wash over her like an unwelcome bucket of lukewarm water. She stared out the window, unsure of what she should feel about her mother coming to help with Lillie.

Relief was one option. Horror was another.

———

"I think it's sweet," Hat protested when Julie opened Genevieve's passenger door and grabbed two of the grocery bags from inside. "She clearly wants to help."

"Hat, you've met my mom, like, once," Julie groaned. "When we put flowers on my dad's grave right after I started working at the PMA. You had to deal with her for half an hour, and even then, you asked to be left in Genevieve while I went in for the barbecue at their house."

"She *is* irritating," Hat conceded.

"Hat, that's my mom you're talking about!" Julie elbowed the door open and made kissy noises at Pookie, who pranced around her feet in delight.

Hat snorted. "You're the one who was just complaining about her coming to stay!"

"She's *my* mom. I can complain about her." Julie groaned, dumping the bags on the kitchen table. "She's going to make me drink that dreadful aloe vera juice."

There was a chiming noise like a doorbell. It took Julie several seconds to realize that it *was* Lillie's doorbell. She was so used to using the back door that she'd forgotten Lille had a front one.

"I'm coming!" she yelled, tossing Hat on the kitchen table. She scooped Pookie into her arms and trotted down the hall past the dusty dining room to the door. It had a little glass peephole, but Julie had no need to use it.

"Oh, *Julia!*" Her mother's voice reverberated down the street. "You didn't water the plants in the front window!"

Julie groaned. She unlocked the door with some effort and

dragged it open, and Mom beamed at her, surrounded by suitcases.

"How long are you planning on staying, Mom?" Julie blurted.

Rosa laughed and threw her arms around Julie, dragging her into a sweaty embrace. "That's my baby girl!" she howled. "Don't you worry, honey. I'll be here as long as it takes." She gave Julie a last squeeze before releasing her. "Grab the big pink case, and I'll bring the others. We'll have to make a second trip for everything else."

Julie maliciously eyed a huge stack of paper-wrapped aloe vera juice bottles. She grabbed the handle of Mom's pink suitcase, which was big enough to hide a body in, and helped her drag it down the hall and into the dining room. She had to lock Pookie in Lillie's bedroom to help Mom lug the rest of her stuff into the house, and the little dog cried the entire time while Lillie's fluffy white cat watched with amusement from his perch on top of a grandfather clock.

"I'm sure we don't need *all* this aloe vera juice," Julie pleaded, dumping a crate of the stuff on the kitchen floor.

"Of course we do, baby. Besides, how else would I supply it to my customers?" Mom smiled. "People rely on me, you know. You should join my company. My whole life has—"

"Mom, I'm not buying into the pyramid scheme, okay?" Julie swatted her hands clean.

To her relief, Rosa was distracted by the groceries on the kitchen table. "Oh, Julia, tell me you don't buy this stuff!" she wailed, pulling out a bottle.

"Ketchup?" Julie raised her eyebrows. "What's wrong with ketchup?"

"This brand is *filled* with additives, honey!" Rosa howled.

Julie tuned her out while she unpacked the rest of the groceries. Her mind raced. *Hat, what am I going to do?* She groaned. *I can't deal with my ketchup choices being criticized for however long!*

Hat snickered unhelpfully.

She was stuffing a box of instant chocolate pudding into the bottom of a kitchen cabinet where Mom wouldn't see it when a siren briefly yipped outside.

"The ambulance is here with Lillie, honey," Mom shouted from the dining room, where she was rearranging the china figures on the mantel for no reason.

Julie's heart leaped. She glanced around the kitchen one last time, hoping Lillie would be happy. Pookie was liberated and bounded down the hall ahead of her as she hurried to the front door, Rosa on her heels. Julie scooped up the dog before she swung the door open.

"Lillie!" she gasped, tears stinging her eyes.

Lillie was leaning on a walker, and her cheeks had lost their pleasant rosy roundness, but her eyes were bright as they met Julie's. "Hello, dear," she murmured, holding out an arm.

"Don't fall." Julie hurried to her side and returned her hug.

"Trust me, it'll take more than a fall to do anything to this old crone," the bearded medic beside Lillie quipped.

Lillie lifted her walker in both hands and brandished it. "I'll do you some damage if you call me a crone again, you young upstart!"

The medic laughed. "Take care of yourself, okay, Lillie? It's been a pleasure."

A second medic stepped out of the cab, carrying Lillie's duffel bag. "Yeah, don't choke and die, you old witch."

Lillie gave the medic an affectionate prod with the walker. "Bye, you two. And Larry?"

The bearded medic looked back. "Yeah?"

"You better go to that bar and ask for that girl's phone number, you hear?" Lillie croaked. "Grow a pair of balls and get on with your life."

"Yes, ma'am!" Larry blushed, saluted, and disappeared into the ambulance.

"What *have* you been doing to the medics, Lillie?" Julie laughed as she held the door open.

Lillie cackled. "Just having a little fun." She tickled Pookie's ears. "Hello, sweetie."

The old lady shuffled into the hallway, and Rosa held out her arms. "Oh, Lillie, it's so good to see you!"

"Rosa!" Lillie returned the woman's hug. "What are you doing here?"

"I'm here to help take care of you, of course." Rosa beamed.

Lillie's smile widened. "Oh, honey, that's so sweet of you. Thank you so much. I'm so glad Julie can share the burden."

"You're not a burden, and you never will be." Julie put a hand on Lillie's back to guide her down the hall into the living room. She'd arranged the coffee table just so: tissues, water, medicine, snacks, the remote, and Lillie's phone charger.

"Look at you, being such a dear." Lillie sank onto the couch with a sigh and patted Julie on the knee.

"I'm making tea!" Rosa bustled into the kitchen.

Julie sat down beside Lillie, searching her face. "How are you feeling?"

"I'm fine, sweetie. Don't worry so much." Lillie squeezed Julie's knee. "I'm going to be okay. It'll take more than a silly cold to put me in the ground. Why, I have to feel Genevieve at full speed again one more time before I die!"

Julie managed a laugh, though the thought made her guts turn inside-out. "As long as you're not driving," she teased.

Lillie cackled. "I said *before* I die, not *when* I die, dear. Now, have you kissed that nice young man yet?"

"What?" Julie's ears turned red-hot.

In her mind, Hat snickered.

"Don't be silly, dear." Lillie leaned back on the couch. "I saw the way he took care of you while I was in the hospital. Always bringing you something to eat, stopping by to say hello, hanging about when he was just getting in the way." She chuckled. "Looks like true love to me."

"Taylor's just a very kind friend, Lillie," Julie protested.

Rosa waddled into the living room, carrying a tray of tea things, and set it on the coffee table. "Are you still pretending that wonderful young specimen is 'just a friend?'" she demanded. "Worse, are you friend-zoning him?"

"How do you know what that is, Mom?" Julie wailed.

Rosa laughed. "I'm middle-aged, not dead, baby."

"Okay, time for a change of subject." Julie grabbed her tea and took a sip. "Urgh! Mom, what is *this*?"

"Rooibos and ginger, honey." Rosa sipped hers.

Julie smacked her lips with deep distaste. It tasted as good as it sounded. "Why?" she croaked.

"You've both spent a lot of time in the hospital with all their superbugs and things, so I thought we could all use an immune booster." Rosa took another deep swig.

Lillie sniffed hers and hastily replaced it on the tray. "Kind of you, Rosa."

Julie stifled a smile. "Lillie, we put my mom's stuff in the dining room for now. I'll take it up to my apartment after lunch."

"Your apartment! Don't be ridiculous, dear. You can hardly fit that handsome young man in there with you as it is." Lillie sniffed.

"Lillie!" Julie moaned.

"Lillie's right, honey. You need your privacy," Rosa told her. "I'll sleep on the couch."

"That's not necessary, dear." Lillie beamed. "There's a spare room. It's been a storeroom for years, but there's a bed and plenty of space for you to make yourself at home."

"See?" Rosa smiled at Julie. "That's settled." She drank more of the tea with every sign of enjoyment, to Julie's horror.

Julie let out a breath. "Thanks, Lillie. That sounds great."

"I'm the one who should be thanking *you*, dear. Both of you."

Lillie squeezed Rosa's hand. "You're being very good friends to a silly old lady."

"You're not silly!" Rosa retorted, beating Julie to it. "Now, who's hungry? I'm making a delicious chicken salad with sunflower seeds and chickpeas."

It seemed like a dodgy combination to Julie, but Lillie beamed. "That sounds wonderful. Thank you, Rosa."

Mom headed back into the kitchen. Julie squeezed Lillie's shoulder. "How about a movie to get settled in again?"

Lillie cackled. "Can we watch one of those with that handsome young bald man?"

"Who?"

"You know, dear. That wrestler. The one with the nice pecs." Lillie gestured at herself, drawing an outline in the air over her elderly chest.

"Dwayne Johnson?" Julie sputtered. She hardly categorized him as young. He was a dad! Then again, the term was relative.

"Yes, *him!*" Lillie leaned back on the sofa. "I think a few minutes of him in a tight t-shirt would do me a world of good."

Julie laughed, set up the movie, and turned it on. Lillie's cat jumped onto her lap and Pookie cuddled up beside her, and the old lady settled into her couch with a smile on her lips. It wasn't long before she let out her first raucous whoop as the car-chasing action heated up.

Shaking her head and chuckling, Julie popped into the kitchen to check on Rosa, who was happily washing lettuce.

Julie glanced at the ingredients set out on the kitchen table. There were three glasses of aloe vera juice poured and ready. She stifled her groan. "Can I help?"

"Sure, honey. You could cut the cucumber for me." Rosa started shredding the lettuce into a bowl.

Julie grabbed the cucumber and fished a knife out of the drawer. "How do you want it?"

"Whichever way you like." Rosa smiled at her. "Lillie looks okay, don't you think?"

"She's still pale." Julie sighed. "I feel so guilty, Mom."

"Don't, baby. You did nothing wrong." Rosa squeezed Julie's wrist with a damp hand. "Lillie's lucky to have you. As lucky as you are to have her."

"Thanks." Julie hesitated. "Mom, thanks for this. Seriously."

Mom looked up, surprised. "For what?"

"For helping me with Lillie. I was scared," Julie admitted. "I didn't know if we could cope alone."

"You know I'm always here for you, baby. Don't you?" Rosa's eyes locked on hers.

Julie smiled. "I do." She meant it. "Thanks for that."

"Any time, honey. Let's finish up this salad and go watch that dreadful action movie." Rosa sighed.

Julie laughed. "Not a *Fast and Furious* fan?"

"I'm more of a *Notting Hill* person," Rosa commented, adding shredded chicken to the bowl.

Julie tossed in the cucumbers and took out some salad dressing. She'd caught Taylor watching the movie on his phone on the flight to Montana, but she'd decided against sharing that information with her mother in case she exploded.

They took their plates of salad into the living room and settled on the couch as the movie went on, with Rosa on one end, Lillie on the other, and Julie in the middle. Lillie whooped as gunshots rattled the windows. Mom winced, and Julie stifled a grin.

She gingerly took a mouthful of the salad. All things considered, it wasn't bad.

CHAPTER SEVENTEEN

Julie hitched her backpack up on her shoulder as she stepped through the doors of the gym at the PMA. "Maybe I could convince the dwarves in the archives to let me hide in the stacks."

Hat scoffed. "I doubt it. Last year, a pixie escaped from the containment unit, and the dwarves tracked it to where it was hiding between the pages of a copy of the *Iliad*."

"Crap. There goes my brilliant plan," Julie grumbled. "How about you turn me into a hat, and I go stay in the SPTM for the next few years?"

"Trust me, it's overrated," Hat told her.

She strode down the hallway, sighing. "Honestly, living with my mother for the first time in a while isn't much better. I can still taste that aloe vera juice she gave us all with our breakfast this morning." She shuddered, remembering how it had washed over her tonsils.

Hat chortled. "Did you see Lillie's face?"

"I thought she was gonna hurl." Julie laughed. "Maybe Lillie and I should take Genevieve and go hide out in Avalon for a while. I'm sure the magical air would sort out Lillie's lungs."

"The mind wipe afterward wouldn't be good for her," Hat pointed out.

"You're a party pooper, Hat." Julie pushed open the gym's doors and headed for the mat in the middle, dumping her backpack beside it. "Okay, here's my best idea yet. You can turn into me, and *you* deal with the two old ladies at home while I sit on *your* head making smartass comments."

Hat snickered. "Oh, no. I'm not giving up my smartass privileges."

"Didn't think so." Julie sighed.

The gym door swung open and Taylor swaggered in, followed by Blake and Teddy. The two Weres grinned at her, and Teddy muttered something in Blake's ear. Blake gave him a good-natured shove with one shoulder.

"Don't they look like trouble," Julie muttered. "Morning, Taylor!"

Taylor grinned as he dropped his duffle bag beside hers. "Good morning."

Julie raised her eyebrows. "What's that supposed to mean?"

"What? I just said good morning!" Taylor raised both hands.

"You said it in a *tone*." Julie folded her arms. "Also, what are these two doing here?"

Taylor's smirk turned into a full-fledged grin. "I thought we'd take your mind off things by making this morning's session extra interesting."

Julie laughed. "Like Friday's session wasn't *interesting* enough for you?" She pulled up her sleeve to inspect the yellowing bruise on her forearm.

Taylor's mouth turned down at the corners. "Hey, don't rub it in. It was an accident."

"No, it was me being an idiot and getting what I deserved." Julie got up and swatted her hands clean against each other. "Now, are we going to start this session or what? I hope you boys are ready to get your asses kicked."

Blake and Teddy exchanged grins. "Yes, ma'am," Blake rumbled.

"I don't think it's *our* asses that are going to get a kicking," Teddy added.

Taylor laughed. "Let's find out."

A moment later, with Hat sitting patiently on Julie's backpack and Teddy watching from a corner, Taylor and Blake circled Julie with their fists raised. Julie kept turning, trying to keep her eye on both, but one kept trying to sneak behind her. She tensed and turned fast. Sweat prickled on her forehead. She hadn't regained the fitness she'd lost after her concussion and Lillie's illness.

"Control the situation. You can't keep an eye on both of us at once," Taylor told her, his chocolate-brown eyes intent on her as he kept his hands near his face. "Break out of the circle. Do something. Str—"

The last word was cut off as Julie lunged at him with a jab and punch. Taylor dodged both and responded with a scything haymaker, which Julie dodged to the left, feeling a whistle of air on her right as Blake attacked with a kick. She threw herself to one knee, and Blake's bare foot flew harmlessly over her head.

She spotted Taylor's feet inches from her. Straining every muscle, Julie swept his legs, knocking her shin hard into his ankles. Taylor stumbled back with a yelp and Julie sprang to her feet, fists raised, and threw a wild punch at Blake as he came at her. It missed, and Blake seized her arm and twisted it.

Muscles sprang tight in Julie's shoulder, complaining, but she didn't tap out. Instead, she moved with the twist, feet quick on the gym mat as she rolled out of the guard and firmly planted an elbow in Blake's stomach. He stumbled back with a cough, grinning.

"Hey, you're learning!" Taylor laughed and bent down to massage his ankles.

Julie gave them a cocky smirk. "I fought a cavern full of Yetis, remember? I think I can handle a couple of idiots in a gym."

"Harsh!" Blake protested.

"I didn't mean it like that." She gave him a friendly punch on the arm.

He chuckled. Taylor shook his head. "Okay, Miss Cocky. Let's try a frontal attack."

"Got it." Julie stepped back, making room on the mat. She focused on Blake and Taylor, who nodded at one another, then rushed her. Taylor's roundhouse kick came from a mile away. Julie dodged it easily, scoffing at him for going easy on her, and grabbed Blake's arm as he punched.

She spun him around and slammed both hands into his ribs, sending him stumbling to the side. Taylor charged her from behind, and as she sidestepped, she heard running feet on the other side of the mat. Julie skittered out of the way instead of turning to attack Taylor, and Teddy stumbled past and crashed into Blake instead of tackling her as he'd planned. The two Weres fell in a heap on the mat, and Taylor grabbed Julie from behind. She tried to plant her feet and wrestle out of his hold, but a strong arm wrapped around her neck, clamping her carotid arteries between a bicep and forearm that felt like cast iron.

"Unnhhh!" Julie grunted. She slapped Taylor's wrist, tapping out.

He let go of her, and her feet touched the floor. "That was pretty good. I like how you made Teddy crash into Blake."

"Dude, what was up with that?" Blake disentangled himself from Teddy.

"You were in the way!" Teddy threw up his arms.

Blake gave his deep, good-natured chuckle and held out a hand to help his shorter friend to his feet.

"Teddy was going to tackle you," Taylor told her, wiping sweat from his brow. "That was the plan, anyway."

"Very sneaky, Mr. Woodskin," Julie teased. "But I'm not sure why you thought you were going to catch me with the same trick that nearly got me killed in the fight with the Yetis."

"Good point." Taylor grinned. "If you hadn't been off-balance, you would have been able to break my rear naked choke."

"Why is it called that? It's kinda inappropriate." Julie bounced on her feet, shaking out the stiffness in her arms.

Taylor shrugged. "I didn't invent the names."

She was panting and bruised in more than one place when her phone's alarm chimed a quarter to nine. Panting, she let go of Blake, who was valiantly trying to get out of her chokehold, and went over to her backpack. "Time to get to work, Taylor."

"Finally." Taylor laughed. "I've been losing my conditioning without you to spar with."

She eyed him. "Clearly."

"Hey!"

After she showered and changed into her work clothes, Julie strolled across the lobby to the elevator, Taylor by her side. She thumbed through her phone. "I have ten messages from Mom as if she didn't talk my ears off at breakfast."

"At least she's helping," Taylor offered.

Julie nodded. "She really is. So, talk to me about ideas for recruiting someone. Do you want to get in touch with Sheila Johnson again? She's had time to think about our offer."

"Mmm, good idea." Taylor smoothed the front of his shirt.

Hat hummed for a moment. "She's still working that low-end construction job. Worth a shot."

"Let's go see her after lunch," Julie suggested. "I'd like to spend the morning—"

Her phone buzzed, and her heart squeezed. She'd set Mom's incoming text tone to a single short buzz so she wouldn't check her phone seven thousand times a day, but it gave two long buzzes. Someone else. *Lillie?* She grabbed her phone, but it was from an unfamiliar number.

Julie, please come to the ER as soon as possible. I would like to go over your blood results with you. Thanks. Dr. Olena

She let out a breath.

"Everything okay?" Taylor asked, pausing beside her halfway across the lobby.

"I think so." Julie dropped her phone back into her pocket. "Dr. Olena wants to see me in the ER about my blood test results."

Taylor's brow furrowed. "Let me come with you."

"Relax, Taylor." Julie laughed. "I'm sure everything is okay. Besides, Kaplan will have your head if you're not in the office by nine."

Taylor sighed. "Okay, but if you need anything, call me. Text me as soon as you know what she says. And if—"

"Okay." Julie shooed him away. "Go on. I'll catch up soon."

She laughed for his benefit as she turned to the front doors, but there was an uncomfortable twinge in the pit of her stomach. She touched the brim of the stylish white cap that she was wearing with her jeans and blouse today. *Do you know what this is about, Hat?*

Hat stirred on her head. *Not a clue. Sorry.*

I guess you're not going to find out for me, either, Julie grumbled.

She stepped out onto the campus and took a deep breath. The sun was gently warm on her skin, although she saw clouds building to the south, and a faint breeze played with her short hair as she walked across the path. It reminded her to take another deep breath. It did little for the knot in her solar plexus.

"Julie! Hey!"

Julie turned. Malcolm jogged up to her, grinning, and she couldn't help but blink and take a step back. "Look at you!"

"Right?" Malcolm laughed and did a little twirl. He wore a snazzy navy suit with a dark blue shirt, although Julie noticed that his black tie had tiny little gray skulls all over it.

Julie laughed. "You look the part of an office grunt."

"I can't believe I haven't seen you since I started working for Uncle Jack." Malcolm folded his arms. "Where have you been?"

"I had to take some personal time. My landlady—well, she's more than a landlady—was very sick."

Malcolm's face fell. "Taylor mentioned it. I'm sorry to hear that."

"She's home now and doing better." Julie smiled. "How are *you* doing? How is life as Kaplan's indentured servant?"

"Don't put it like that. It's too close to the truth." Malcolm groan-laughed. "Uncle Jack can be very demanding. Where are you hurrying off to?"

"I need to follow up on some stuff from my physical at the medical unit." Julie kept her tone airy.

"Let me walk you over there. I can tell you're in a hurry."

"Thanks." Julie let out a breath. "That would be nice."

"I'm always nice." Malcolm batted his eyelashes.

Julie playfully swatted at him as they trudged across the grass. "Yeah, except when you try to mesmerize innocent people who are trying to rescue you."

Malcolm groaned. "Can you let that go? I apologized, and you *did* slap me for it."

"Just don't forget that I've saved your life twice, Malcolm Nox." Julie smirked. "So, spill the beans. How is life as a working stiff?"

"In all honesty, I'm enjoying it." Malcolm laughed. "Uncle Jack is strict, but it feels like I have something to get up for in the mornings. Besides, Cassidy's been much more chill since I started working. She's always nagged me to 'do something with my life.'" He enclosed the latter in air quotes.

Good for you, Cassidy. Julie kept that thought to herself. "Marriage and a job in one week. Must be a shock to the system."

"A little." Malcolm shrugged. "A good shock, though. I mean, I haven't rushed off to go do weird shit like chase down Yetis for a while."

"A while?" Julie raised an eyebrow. "It's been little more than a week."

"Yeah, yeah." Malcolm laughed. "Anyway, it feels good to get out of bed in the mornings for more than just another FPS game."

The ER loomed over them, and Julie turned to Malcolm. "I've got to go. You don't want to be late. Dear old Uncle Jack doesn't like that."

Malcolm's eyes widened. "Don't call him 'dear old Uncle Jack.' He'll throw a bus."

"I've heard that before." Julie snorted. "See you around."

"See you, Julie. Oh, and Cassidy asked you to dinner sometime this week. If you'd like to come."

Julie grinned. "I'd love to. Thanks."

Malcolm hustled off at a jog, checking his phone for the time. Julie was left alone to face whatever Dr. Olena wanted to tell her so urgently. She squared her shoulders and went to face the music.

The glass doors slid open, and Julie strode into the ER. Dr. Olena was standing by the reception desk, flipping through some paperwork on a clipboard with a frown on her face. She paused on one of the papers and her frown deepened, her mouth twisting sideways as she chewed the inside of her cheek.

"Hey, Doc," Julie chirped. "What's up?"

Dr. Olena looked up, her blue eyes catching on Julie's face. "Thanks for coming so quickly. There's something I need to talk to you about."

Julie managed a laugh. "Hello to you too."

Dr. Olena didn't respond. She hurried into a private room and Julie followed, heart thudding behind her breastbone. *What's going on?* She found herself looking down at her hands as she walked, turning them this way and that. They looked fine. Normal. She wasn't dying, was she?

She swallowed hard. Of course she wasn't dying. That was crazy.

If Hat was listening to her inner turmoil, he didn't offer any comments. Dr. Olena closed the door behind them and turned to face Julie after setting the clipboard on the bed.

"Julie, I—" she began.

"This is going to be interesting."

Julie and the Sylthana Elf both jumped. Whipping around, Julie saw that the Sphynx—Horusiris-blah-blah-blah—was sitting on the pillow, licking his paws.

"Where did *you* come from?" Dr. Olena blurted.

The Sphynx blinked. "The aether, darling. I *am* a Sphynx."

"What do you mean, 'this is going to be interesting?'" Julie demanded.

The Sphynx blinked again, then returned to washing his paws.

"Okay, nope." Dr. Olena opened the door. "Out. Now."

"Excuse you, madam. I'm a high-ranking member of the OPMA," the Sphynx purred.

"Yeah? Well, firstly, that's 'doctor' to you," Dr. Olena shot back, "and also, Julie has a right to privacy in a medical setting."

The Sphynx sighed. "I don't have an answer for that, do I?" He looked at Julie, and she could swear he was smirking, revealing sharp little white teeth. "Very well, *Doctor*. She'll find out soon anyway."

He leaped off the bed and stalked out the door with his tail in the air, taking his sweet time. Dr. Olena closed the door behind him as though that would keep him out of the room. "I'm sorry about that." She turned back to Julie. "I need to redo your blood tests."

"Why?" Julie swallowed hard. "Is something wrong? Am I sick?"

"Sick? No!" Dr. Olena shook her head, her silver hair whipping over her shoulders. "Don't worry about that. It's just... well, something's not adding up."

"What do you mean?" Julie asked. "Is it my DNA like you mentioned last time?"

"Something like that." Dr. Olena opened a drawer and took out a tourniquet and a blood tube. "Sorry again."

Julie shrugged and sat down. The mad thudding of her heart had eased. "No worries, Doc. As long as I'm not in trouble."

"If Kaplan gives you any lip, tell him to come to me." Dr. Olena winked and wrapped the tourniquet around Julie's arm. The needle slipped into her vein so gently that she barely felt it, and Dr. Olena filled a tube with her blood.

Julie glanced around the room. *I'm pretty sure that not seeing the Sphynx doesn't mean he's not here.*

Hat snorted. *No comment.*

What do you mean, "no comment?" What's your deal with the Sphynxes? Julie grouched.

There's no "deal" with the Sphynxes, Hat retorted.

Julie scoffed. *Uh-huh. I'm sure there isn't.*

Don't be sarcastic with me, Julia.

"Julie?"

Julie blinked. "Sorry, Doc. What was that?"

"I said, would you mind coming down to the lab with me?" Dr. Olena smiled, but her eyes were serious.

"To the lab?" Julie raised an eyebrow. "Sure, but why?"

Dr. Olena held up the blood tube. "Just for interest's sake. I'm going to run the bloods myself. I want to make sure they're accurate this time."

"This time?" Julie echoed.

CHAPTER EIGHTEEN

Dr. Olena didn't respond, just hurried off. Julie followed her deeper into the medical unit. After taking a few tight turns in the cool network of hallways, they ended up in a large, pale room filled with whirring machines and complex equipment.

Julie recognized some of the machines—a scanning electron microscope, a centrifuge, and a DNA sequencer—but others were unfamiliar. There was an enormous treadmill, twice the size of an ordinary one, with glass walls around it. One wall was taken up by a huge glass tank full of water, while something that looked like an MRI machine the size of a dollhouse sat on the end of one of the tables.

Julie picked up a small object lying on one of the tables. It looked like an infrared thermometer but had a probe with a circular section sticking out of it. "What's this thing?"

"A thaumometer," Dr. Olena murmured. She clipped one of the samples into the machine that looked like a DNA sequencer.

"What does it do?" Julie considered pointing it at herself.

"Measures the amount of magic in your blood," Dr. Olena explained. "Not good for the ego in general."

Julie hastily replaced the thaumometer on the table. "This must be an MRI machine for pixies."

Dr. Olena was poking the sequencer's screen. "I use it for weremice too."

"This thing clearly isn't for weremice." Julie indicated the glass-sided treadmill.

Dr. Olena glanced up. "That's a water treadmill for equids. You know, centaurs, unicorns, pegasi. Good for resistance training and stress tests. Please don't touch it. It cost eighty thousand dollars."

Julie retreated and went to stand by Dr. Olena and the sequencer. The Sylthana Elf pressed a button on the screen, and the sequencer made a hissing sound.

"Doesn't this take forever?" Julie asked.

Dr. Olena grinned. "It does unless you give it supernatural help." She pressed both hands to the sequencer, and its hiss grew more intense. Closing her eyes, the Sylthana Elf bowed her head, and blue light played around her fingers as her magic coursed into the machine.

Shit, that's cool. Julie sighed.

Hat said nothing. She tugged gently on his crown. *Hello? Anyone home?*

Yeah, yeah, Hat grunted.

Why are you so quiet? Julie demanded. *It's weird.*

Hat didn't respond. Julie's stomach knotted again. If he knew something, why wasn't he telling her? Was something horribly wrong?

Dr. Olena sat back, and the machine gave a last hiss and printed a report. The doctor grabbed the paper out of the printer and read it quickly, her frown intensifying. It was gibberish to Julie, just rows of letters. She assumed they were her DNA sequence.

Dr. Olena let out a huff and tossed the paper on the table.

"No, no!" she burst out. "That can't be right. We need to run this *again*."

Julie bit her lip. "Is something wrong?"

Dr. Olena flashed her a quick smile. "No, you're fine. I just...I think the settings on this machine aren't calibrated for human DNA. Have you ever been DNA-tested by human medicine?"

"No." Julie bit her lip. "Doc, do I have a horribly disfiguring genetic disease or something?"

Dr. Olena shook her head, but her smile was still distracted, and her eyes were worried. She held up the tourniquet again, and Julie submitted to having yet another blood sample taken and slipped into the DNA sequencer. Dr. Olena was silent for a long time as she held her hands to the machine.

Julie's stomach felt as though it was trying to climb up her chest.

Hat, help me out, she muttered.

Hat said nothing. Julie gave him a sharp tug to check if he was still alive, and he jumped. *Ow!*

Come on, say something, Julie grumbled.

Dr. Olena sat back and looked at the new printout, then at Julie, then at the printout again. Raising an elegant forefinger to her mouth, she nibbled on the nail, her frown deepening.

Julie took a step closer, hands on her hips. "Okay, Dr. Olena. Enough with the cryptic answers. Just tell me what's going on."

The Sylthana Elf took a deep breath, looked at the printout, and finally met Julie's eyes. "I don't understand what's going on," she admitted. "According to these tests, you're not human."

The world tipped under Julie's feet. She grabbed the edge of the table to stay upright. "What? How? I mean, that can't be right. The sequencer must be wrong like you said."

"I don't know. I doubt it." Dr. Olena groaned. "It shouldn't be giving me these results, Julie. It doesn't make sense."

"What results?" Julie squawked.

Dr. Olena held up the printout and gestured at the gibberish, eyes wild. "The test is correct. It must be. It's telling me you're not human."

Julie sagged into a chair near Dr. Olena's, pulled Hat into her lap, and ran a hand through her hair.

The Sphynx appeared out of thin air and stepped onto Dr. Olena's table. He stretched luxuriously, knocking the thaumometer off the table with his hind paws as he did so, and turned to face the Sylthana Elf.

"That's because she isn't."

Julie's ears filled with a distant buzz. Dr. Olena was saying something while glaring at the Sphynx, who was licking his bare flanks. She didn't hear anything. Hat squirmed in her lap like he was talking to her too, but her head was filled with static.

That and the image of her parents. Mom. Dad. Mom with her rambunctious personality. Dad with his kind eyes. She had Dad's nose. She was human. She was Dad's girl. She could hear him saying that when she was twelve years old, and he took her to the retirement home to give Christmas gifts to all the lonely old people.

She'd left with tears in her eyes for the sad old man who had rejected her gifts and sat in a corner all alone. Dad had wrapped her in his arms and kissed her forehead. *Never lose your heart, Julie. That's my girl.* She could *hear* his words echoing in her mind. She was Dad's girl, and whether she liked it or not, she was Mom's girl too. Maybe she could imagine Dad being some kind of epic paranormal, but Mom was as human as anyone could possibly be.

What was she even thinking? She gave herself a shake. Of course she was human. Every paranormal she'd ever met except dear old Leafeyes and Palladius had immediately commented on it.

"Julie?" Dr. Olena had gripped her hand. "Julie, are you okay?"

She raised her head, swallowing hard. "What do you mean I'm not human?" The words croaked out through a mouth that felt bone-dry. "What *am* I, then?"

"It's too early to say." Dr. Olena sat back. "All I know is that the assumption that you had the genetic mutation that allows humans to see our world was wrong. I can prove you don't have the gene." She paused. "There's only one explanation. You must be a paranormal."

"I don't look like one. No one has ever thought I was one," Julie protested.

Dr. Olena shrugged and held up her hands. "I don't know, Julie. I don't have the answers right now. I need to run a bunch more tests before I can tell you anything concrete."

Julie glanced around. "Where's the Sphynx? He must know."

"He disappeared," Hat told her. "Typical."

"Don't you snark on the Sphynx, Hat." Julie picked him up and held him at eye level, looking him firmly in the brim. "You knew about this, didn't you? What am I?"

Hat hesitated. "I couldn't say."

"Why didn't you tell me?"

"I couldn't!" Hat spat, his voice cracking.

Julie lowered him back to her lap, nausea roiling in her gut. She looked at Dr. Olena. "What now?" Her lips felt numb as they folded around the words.

"I'm going to keep working on this, and I'll consult other physicians in the paranormal world." Dr. Olena picked up the tourniquet again. "I'm afraid I need to treat you like a pincushion again. I'm going to take a bunch more blood and send it to labs in Avalon and the human world to confirm my test."

Julie nodded as Dr. Olena slipped the tourniquet around her arm. "Doc, do I have patient confidentiality?"

"Of course you do." Dr. Olena inserted the needle into her

vein. "Not even Kaplan will know until you feel it's the right time to tell him."

"Okay." Julie sucked in a trembling breath. *Maybe this is all a mistake. A whole different genetic mutation.* She looked down at her boring, ordinary hands that didn't have any magic in them and couldn't transform into a different being and felt marginally better. She *was* human. She had to be. Being a paranormal didn't make sense.

Dr. Olena had several tubes on the table beside her when she was through. She unclipped the tourniquet and put a Band-Aid over the puncture in the crook of Julie's elbow. "It's a good thing you have lovely veins." She smiled. "I promise I'll get to the bottom of this, Julie. Try not to worry in the meantime. It doesn't make sense to obsess over it when we don't have any answers."

Julie rubbed her arm. "Easier said than done, Doc."

"I know." Dr. Olena grimaced. "I'm sorry, but like I said, I'll get you your answers."

"Thanks." Julie got up. "Any idea when you'll know?"

"I'll keep you updated, but it depends on how many different tests I need to run to figure out what's happening." Dr. Olena shrugged. "Don't worry. The rest of your blood tests show that you're in excellent health—whatever you are—and I see plenty of paras who would give their eyeteeth to be able to say the same."

Paras. Was she one of them? *I can't be.* Julie tugged her sweatshirt down over her elbow again. "Thanks for your help."

"Anytime." Dr. Olena grinned. "Now go and eat something high in protein, followed by a generous dessert."

Julie raised an eyebrow. "Are you suggesting, as a medical doctor, that I should eat my feelings?"

The Sylthana Elf smirked. "Just this once."

The excellent fresh rainbow trout with lemon stuffing would have been better with a touch of garlic, but it was good enough to take Julie's mind off her conversation with Dr. Olena for a little while. It was only when the last forkful of the fish had melted in her mouth and she was standing in line for dessert that the questions began to accumulate in her mind again.

Her phone buzzed. Mom, of course. She checked the text.

You forgot to pack your lunchtime juice.

Her lip twitched, but as she dropped the phone back into her pocket, Julie felt a cold hand clutch at her guts. Mom. She was human, right? She didn't even know about the paranormal world.

Maybe I'm like Ellie, Julie considered, thinking about the half-human, half-Woodland Fae who'd been her first recruit. She straightened Hat on her head. *Come on, Hat. Do you seriously have nothing to say?*

I'm sorry this is happening to you. Hat's crown tightened around her head. *It's a shock.*

A shock! Julie scoffed and looked over her dessert options. *I've just found out I might not be the* species *I think I am. It's more than a shock.* She chose a decadent chocolate mousse and asked for extra cream.

You're still you, Hat told her. *Whether you're human or not, you're still Julie Meadows. That will never change.*

Aw, thanks, Hat. Julie took her mousse to the table and sat down, then shoveled in a mouthful of the fluffy, chocolatey goodness. *I just don't understand. I know I'm not adopted. I've seen pictures of my exhausted-looking mom holding ugly, purple newborn me. But they're both human. They have to be.*

I don't have answers for you, Hat murmured.

Julie took another bite of her mousse. *I'm sorry I was sharp to you earlier. I was, uh, stressed.*

I don't blame you. Hat paused. *Are you going to tell Kaplan?*

Not right now. Julie sat back in her chair and closed her eyes to savor the glorious mousse sliding down her throat.

What about Taylor? Hat asked.

Before she could answer, footsteps echoed down the hall. Julie opened her eyes. It was Taylor, and his hair was on end as he ran into the almost empty room. It wasn't a popular spot at ten o'clock in the morning.

"There you are!" he blurted. "What are you doing?"

"Dr. Olena had to take a bunch more blood." Julie held up her mousse. "Doctor's orders."

Taylor glanced at her, brow furrowing. "Is everything okay? You're not..." He stopped.

Human, Julie thought. *I'm not human.* She pushed it aside. "Sick? No. Everything's fine. She just needed to do a lot of tests."

"Good." Taylor's shoulders slumped, then he jumped like he had been electrocuted. "We've got to go! Kaplan is losing his shit."

"What about?" Julie raised an eyebrow.

"I don't know. All he said was, 'Briefing! *Now!*'" Taylor peered at her. "Come *on!*"

He dashed out, and Julie sighed. She grabbed her dessert and ran out the door after him.

AUTHOR NOTES RENÉE JAGGÉR

JANUARY 4, 2023

Thank you for reading through to the back of book three!

I'm in Arizona. Again. Surprise, right? We spent a lovely holiday season here, Jo and me, and the mountains are covered with snow, even if there is none on the ground. As much of a white Christmas as we usually get!

We did get a white New Year's. It rained and hailed and had a good ol' time for itself. I was tucked up tight, making excellent slow-cooker corn chowder and my new passion, no-knead bread. Have you heard of it? If not, check out the recipe on the web at https://www.kingarthurbaking.com/recipes/no-knead-crusty-white-bread-recipe.

It's the best, and it literally takes five minutes to make. The New Year's version featured kalamata olives, but we have made rye, rosemary, and cheese varieties at other times. It's especially wonderful made into garlic bread with the good Irish butter, and the neighbors love you when you bring them some.

Versatile and delicious! Jo gives it two dewclaws up!

The spiked eggnog was great too, and I watched *Knives Out* again and then *Glass Onion*. Give yourself a treat if you haven't seen them.

I also caught the mead habit while I was in the UK, so friends and I made some for Christmas. It's burbling away in a closet, smelling great, and I can't wait to taste our creation. We made a pretty basic recipe, but there are all kinds.

Next on the docket is cyser, which is made with unfiltered apple cider and honey and raisins. That should taste like a combination of mead and hard cider, another favorite. Such a lovely spring coming up! These have to perk for a month or two, but then we can taste them. Then we bottle the whole shebang and let it age. We'll make some metheglin, spiced cider, in time to have it age at least six months for next holiday season. Everyone is looking forward to that!

I make this sound like I am an alcoholic, but the reality is I drink one small glass, and I'm snoring. Therefore, I want the best I can get in that glass, and since I don't drink the hard stuff, I can play with making my own. Here's a toast to hoping our new mead venture provides that best! Oh, wait! We finished the bottle I brought back from the UK. Oh, well. I'll just have to wait until this batch is ready.

Back to Christmas. I made the mistake of mentioning to someone that I have always wanted to learn to fly a helicopter, so guess who got a lesson certificate in their stocking? I can't wait! Vegas can truly provide whatever one wants. I know a certain publisher whose initials are MA who drove a Ferrari on a track there.

I shall report on my experience after I schedule and take the lesson. *That's* going to end up in a book, for sure!

The next book is already with the publisher. As always, thank you to my proofreaders! They make my books the best they can be. I hope you enjoyed the continuation of Julie's journey! Her world will keep changing, as will she.

Until we speak again, I hope your skies are sunny and your days are filled with happiness and good books!

Renée

BOOKS FROM RENÉE

Para-Military Recruiter
(with Michael Anderle)
Drafted (Book 1)
Recruiter (Book 2)
Accepted (Book 3)
Lead (Book 4)

Reincarnation of the Morrigan
Birth of a Goddess (Book One)
The Way of Wisdom (Book Two)
Angelic Death (Book Three)
A Cold War (Book 4)
A Battle Tune (Book 5)
Broken Ice (Book 6)
A Torn Veil (Book 7)
Sins of the Past (Book 8)
The Wild Hunt Comes (*coming soon*)

The WereWitch Series
Bad Attitude (Book One)

A Bit Aggressive (Book Two)
Too Much Magic (Book Three)
Were War (Book Four)
Were Rages (Book Five)
God Ender (Book Six)
God Trials (Book Seven)
The Troll Solution (Book Eight)
Winner Takes All (Book Nine)

Callie Hart Series
Thin Ice (Book One)
Cold Blood (Book Two)
Feelings Run Deep (Book Three)

BOOKS BY MICHAEL ANDERLE

Sign up for the LMBPN email list to be notified of new releases and special deals!

https://lmbpn.com/email/

For a complete list of books by Michael Anderle, please visit:

www.lmbpn.com/ma-books/

CONNECT WITH THE AUTHORS

Connect with Renée

Facebook: https://www.facebook.com/reneejaggerauthor

Website: https://reneejagger.com/

Connect with Michael Anderle

Website: http://lmbpn.com

Email List: https://michael.beehiiv.com/

https://www.facebook.com/LMBPNPublishing

https://twitter.com/MichaelAnderle

https://www.instagram.com/lmbpn_publishing/

https://www.bookbub.com/authors/michael-anderle